45 3028218 6

KT-551-863

A few minutes later, the others arrived. Jack and Kemal jumped up to greet them.

'Thought you must have got lost,' said Jack. 'We've been up the mountain and back while we were waiting.'

'Liar!' said Daz, dancing like a boxer in front of him.

Jack dodged about, imitating Daz, laughing. Then he leapt back.

'Hey! Careful!' shouted Mike.

But his warning was too late. As Jack's feet landed back on the ground he felt the loose stones shift beneath them and before he could do anything to stop himself, he was over the edge and beginning to slide down the hillside.

Look out for other titles in the *Go For It!* series:

You Can Do It!

Jill Atkins

WATFORD REGIONAL COLLEGE LIBRARY
WARD CENTRE

CONTROL No 203843

4330282186
8 23114 ATIC (T-REND)

PRICE 2.99   DATE 08/07

Evans Brothers Limited

Published by Evans Brothers Limited
2A Portman Mansions
Chiltern Street
London W1U 6NR

© Copyright Jill Atkins, 2003

First published 2003

All rights reserved. No part of this publication may be reproduced, stored in a retrieval system or transmitted in any form or by any means, electronic, mechanical, photocopying, recording or otherwise, without prior permission of Evans Brothers Limited.

British Library Cataloguing in Publication Data
Atkins, Jill
You can do it!. - (Go for it!)
1. Children's stories
I. Title
823.9'14 [J]

ISBN 0237525798

Series Editor: Julia Moffatt
Designer: Jane Hawkins

The author would like to thank the Spinal Injuries Association and the Spinal Injuries Unit at Stoke Mandeville Hospital for their advice.

Chapter One

It was almost the end of the match and Jack's team was one up. His best mate, Daz, had the ball. Jack saw him loft it high over the heads of the defenders. He watched the ball keenly as he ran into a space. Down it came right onto his boot. It felt as though some extra-terrestrial force had touched him and a great surge raced up his legs and through his body. He left the rest of them for dead. Left foot, right foot, he dribbled the ball towards the goal. He side-stepped one defender, two defenders, as the ball skidded and bobbled over the rough pitch.

Out of the corner of his eye, he noticed Lara and Brook, two girls from his form, on the touchline.

'Come on, Jack!' they screamed.

'Come on, Jack!' he echoed inside his brain. 'You can do it!'

'Stop him!' yelled a boy from the opposing team.

Jack sensed the boot homing in towards the side of his ankle, but he was perfectly balanced and leapt over the challenge. They weren't going to get him so easily. Now there was only the goalie to beat, but Jack was not going to let a little shrimp like that get in his way.

He raised his eyes for a split second and sized up the goal. The posts seemed miles apart. He couldn't miss! With barely a pause, his left foot met the ball a few centimetres from the mud on the edge of the area. Whack! Thwack! The ball shot with the speed of light into the back of the net.

'Goal!' The roar resounded deafeningly in his head. He was in the new Olympic Stadium playing for England. He had just scored the winning goal in the World Cup Final! He leapt high and punched the air.

'Yes!' he yelled as seven or eight of his team-mates surged on to him, hugging him and thumping him on the back.

'No kisses!' he shouted and pursed his lips at Daz, who was clinging to him like a limpet.

'Ugh!' Daz's arms relaxed and he sprang away from Jack. He laughed loudly as he ran off up the pitch with the others.

Jack felt ten feet tall. It may not be the World Cup, but it *was* the last match of the season, the decider in the Schools Under 15s challenge and he *had* scored twice. *And* that second goal had put them into a commanding lead.

'How long to go?' he called to Mr Oakley, who was dashing up and down the touchline.

His PE teacher consulted his watch.

'Five minutes,' he called. 'Time for one or two more?'

'At least three,' Jack said, as he flexed his leg muscles a few metres from the line. 'How about a volley, a banana bender from the corner and a Beckham free kick?'

'With your cheek, I wouldn't put it past you!' chuckled Mr Oakley.

'No, but *I'll* put it past the goalie!' called Jack as the whistle blew for the restart and he sprinted away.

A quarter of an hour later, after one more goal, Jack and his mates were in the changing room, almost ready to leave.

'Stunning hat trick!' said Kemal. 'I wish I had your golden boots.'

'Yeah,' said Daz. 'You were fantastic!'

'Thank you, fans!' Jack bowed low. He grinned. 'Do you reckon the England scouts were out there looking for talent?'

'That's one thing I like about you, Jack Wallis,' said Daz, giving Jack a punch on the shoulder. 'You're so modest with it!'

'Your passes weren't so bad,' said Jack, pulling on his trainers. 'But I've got to start somewhere if I'm playing for England in the 2010 World Cup.'

'Ooo!' laughed Daz. 'Aim high, why don't you?'

'Why not?' said Jack.

'Hurry up, you lads!' called Mr Oakley from the doorway.

'Hey, Mr Oakley!' called Jack. 'Why is the school football pitch always so soggy?'

'Well...' began Mr Oakley.

'Because the players are always dribbling!' said Jack.

Mr Oakley laughed.

'Haven't you got homes to go to?' he asked.

'For the time being,' said Jack. He put on his coat. 'Just until I'm spirited away to the Premier League. Then I'll live in a palace!'

'Good job I know you're really a decent unassuming lad!' said Mr Oakley. 'Now clear off, *please*, so I can go home myself!'

'He's all right, old Oakley,' said Jack when the teacher had gone. 'He can take it.'

'He's used to you by now,' said Kemal, picking up his bag.

'Yeah, he must need his brains testing,' said Daz. 'Come on. Let's go.'

They raced each other through the school gates and along the road.

'See you,' said Jack when they reached the corner of his street. Then he sauntered home.

'Great goals, Jack!'

Jack turned. It was Lara. She must have been waiting for him. He smiled to himself. *She fancies me*, he thought.

'Thanks!' he called, but he couldn't be bothered to stop to talk so he waved and smiled and hurried on. One day, when he had made it to the top, he would have time for Lara. There would be loads of girlfriends. They'd all be after him then!

'I scored a hat trick,' he shouted as he burst in the back door. 'The first goal was a gem. I was in the penalty area and...'

'Boring!' moaned Emma. She was sitting at the kitchen table with a large book open in front of her.

' ...and I dodged past four of five defenders...'

' Go away!'

' ...and I hit the perfect volley...'

'Shut up, little brother! Can't you get it into your pea-sized brain that some people aren't actually interested in a load of silly boys kicking something around in the mud?'

'You'll eat your words when I'm world famous and unbelievably rich.'

Emma pulled a face.

'You're pathetic,' she said. 'What chance have you got of ever getting further than the school team?'

'You haven't seen me play!'

'And I don't want to either! Anyway, clear off and disturb someone else, will you? Can't you see I'm trying to get this project finished?'

'Project?' said Jack. '*Now* who's being boring?'

Emma frowned and thrust her hands on her hips.

'You may be aware that I'm taking my GCSEs,' she said.

'Who needs those?' asked Jack. 'Once I'm taken on by Man U or Arsenal I'll—'

'—you'll be just as big a pain in the bottom.'

'All right, all right, I can take a hint. I'm going!'

Jack hurried from the kitchen and slammed the door behind him.

'Is that you, Jack?' Mrs Wallis called from the front room. 'How did you get on?'

'It was brilliant!' said Jack as he followed the sound and found her sitting with her feet up.

'I've had one heck of a bad day at work,' she groaned. 'Come and tell me about your game.'

At least his mum listened to him even when she had had a hard day.

'Wow!' she said when he had finished describing his goals. 'I don't know how your team would survive without you!'

'Don't be sarcastic!' Jack said, pulling a face. 'You know you're dead proud of me, really. Hey, what time's Dad in tonight?'

'About 6.30, I expect. He'll take you to ATC, if you want.'

Jack grinned. His mum had read his mind, as usual. There weren't many secrets you could keep from her. She always seemed to know. Dad wasn't that bad either, as dads go.

'And Jack,' Mrs Wallis said quietly. 'Try not to wind your sister up quite so much. She's taking her exams very seriously. Let her do her work in peace, will you? I wish more of my children were interested in doing well for themselves.'

'Hey! That's not fair!' said Jack. 'I happen to be very interested in doing well for myself.'

Just then the door opened and Craig breezed in and sat down. Craig always seemed to have his eyes focused on the TV or the computer screen or some new game on his Game Boy.

'Hi,' said Mrs Wallis. 'How was school today?'

Craig grunted and picked up the remote control.

'Got much homework?'

Craig grunted again and stared at the TV.

'Hey, square eyes!' called Jack. 'Can I have a go on your Game Boy?'

Craig shook his head. He waved the remote control at the TV. Some kids' programme came on. Jack couldn't stand it. He stood up to leave. In spite of having a go at

Emma, he knew he had to get his homework finished before he went out.

An hour later, they were eating at the kitchen table. Mr Wallis had just arrived home.

'Had a good day?' he asked as he sat down.

'Yeah, great,' said Jack. 'I scored a hat trick.'

'Well done,' said Mr Wallis.

'Me and Kemal and Daz make a great team. They feed me good crosses and...'

'Oh, you mean to say that you weren't the only one on the pitch?' Emma butted in sarcastically. 'From the way you were talking earlier...'

'You're only jealous...'

'You've got to be joking!'

'You two!' said Mr Wallis. 'Don't you ever stop going at each other?'

Jack threw a dirty look at Emma and she stuck her tongue out. Mr Wallis turned to Craig.

'What about you, Craig?' he asked. 'You're a bit quiet.'

'That's not surprising,' complained Craig. 'I can't get a word in with these two always making such a din.'

Jack leaned towards his dad.

'But it was a great match...' he said.

'Is it next week you go to North Wales?' Mrs Wallis interrupted.

'Yeah, can't wait!' said Jack.

'Nor can I,' sighed Emma. 'I'll have peace and quiet for a whole week!'

'Yeah!' said Craig.

Air Training Corps was Jack's second most favourite thing after football, although some of it was actually very boring, like when they had to go on parade and march up and down. But the rest was amazing. They had done gliding, canoeing, abseiling, flying, orienteering and all sorts of other great activities. And they were going away for a whole week in the Easter holidays, camping in Snowdonia. It was going to be brilliant.

Chapter Two

The next few days passed slowly for Jack. The end of term arrived and there was nothing to do now that football training had stopped for the season. To make matters worse, it rained solidly for three days and he was forced to hang around at home, bored.

Emma was still revising for her exams. Jack went to her room and pushed open the door, made a face at her then kicked one of her cuddly toys in the air. Emma rolled her eyes and sighed.

'Why can't you go away, go round to Daz's, go jump in the lake, anything!' she shouted. 'You're always in my space!'

'And you're always so boring!'

'And you're always a flaming nuisance!' Emma yelled, throwing her pen at him. 'Why do I have to put up with such a pain as you? Get out of my room!'

'OK, sister!' said Jack in an American accent. 'This place sure isn't big enough for the both of us.'

'You're telling me!'

Jack went to find Craig. It was easy. He just had to follow the bleeping sounds. Craig didn't even seem to notice when Jack breezed into his bedroom. He was playing with his Game Boy as usual.

'Can I have a go?' asked Jack.

No answer.

'Hey! Craig!'

'What?' Craig muttered keeping his eyes on the game.

'Oh, nothing.'

It wasn't worth it. He went downstairs. It had finally stopped raining so he hurried out into the garden with his football.

At last, the day arrived and Jack was sitting in the back of the minibus on his way to the mountains of North Wales. There were eight of them altogether – himself, Daz and Kemal, three other boys and Mike and Tony, the leaders, plus all their gear. Mike was driving.

'Have a lovely time,' his mum had said as they left. 'Don't do anything foolish.'

The journey seemed to last forever, but they all chatted away and cracked jokes and everyone stayed cheerful.

'Hey! What's that copper doing up that tree?' Jack asked, pointing out of the window.

'We don't know,' said Kemal. 'What *is* that copper doing up that tree?'

'He's working for special branch!' said Jack.

Everyone laughed.

They reached the hills of North Wales. Every field was dotted with thousands of sheep and lambs.

'Hey, where do you put a criminal sheep?' asked Jack.

'We don't know,' said Daz. 'Where *do* you put a criminal sheep?'

'Behind baas!'

They all laughed again. Jack felt good. This was going to be a fantastic week.

Finally, they arrived at the campsite and unloaded the van. Jack, Kemal and Daz threw themselves into the job of erecting tents. After a few tangles and minor disasters, they stood back and admired their work. Then Jack helped unpack the cooking equipment and lit a fire. He and Mike were first on cooking duty. It was burgers and beans for supper.

Kemal was sent to collect wood for the fire and Daz went for water. By the time they returned, a delicious smell rose from the pans.

'I'm starving,' said Daz. 'Will my burger be long?'

'No,' said Jack. 'It'll be round, like everyone else's!'

'Don't you ever stop?' asked Mike with a broad grin across his face.

'Not very often,' said Kemal.

That night, they hardly slept a wink. It was always like

this on the first night of camp. Everyone was too excited, calling from tent to tent, nipping out in the dark to find the toilet tent, cracking jokes and guffawing loudly. Mike and Tony gave up telling them to be quiet. It was almost four o'clock when silence fell and even Jack felt himself relax into sleep.

Later that morning, Jack woke to hear water dripping outside the tent. It was raining. He couldn't believe it. It had rained enough for the whole year over the past few days. When he pushed his head through the tent flap and peered bleary-eyed outside, all he could see was a white swirling mist and large muddy puddles.

'We can't venture anywhere until this fog clears,' said Mike.

Jack felt disappointed and frustrated. He had been waiting for this moment for so long and now there was another delay, but he slid out of his sleeping bag, had a very quick wash in cold water and got dressed. He wanted to be ready the moment the weather improved.

'I've just heard the weather forecast,' said Mike at breakfast, which they ate huddled together inside the biggest tent. 'It should be OK by lunchtime.'

That news made Jack feel better immediately.

'Let's hope they've got it right, for once,' he said. 'Knowing them, it'll probably be snowing!'

Luckily, the rain stopped mid-morning and they found the driest patch of ground for a quick game of football. The first gap in the clouds appeared as they were eating sandwiches at midday. Jack was standing on a rock, staring up at the hills, which seemed to grow higher and higher as the clouds lifted.

'The mountains go on forever,' he shouted to Daz and Kemal, who were a few metres away on other rocks. 'Which one do you think is Everest?'

'Ha! Ha!' said Daz.

After lunch, they dressed in warm gear and heavy walking shoes and packed small rucksacks with drinks, chocolate bars, whistles, torches and maps.

'We've only got a few hours of daylight left,' called Mike, when they were ready. 'We must keep up a good pace over the lower slopes if we want to tackle some of the real stuff today.'

Jack hopped from one foot to the other. He was so eager to start.

'And it's vital that you all watch your step,' said Mike as they set off. 'There's been heavy rain lately and there'll be a lot of loose stones in places.'

'OK, boss,' said Jack.

He swung his arms and breathed deeply as they strode out along the wet, well-trodden track, which rose slowly towards the mountain. He felt a strong buzz of excitement.

It wasn't the same feeling as when he was scoring goals, but it was the thought of 'tackling some of the real stuff', as Mike had put it, that attracted him. He had joked about Everest, but at the moment, Mount Snowdon was enough of a challenge.

'Today, Snowdon, tomorrow, Everest!' he said to himself.

Then, as they came round a bend, he saw the mountain, its top still hidden in a crown of white cloud. He shivered. It looked very high even though he knew it was like a pimple compared to mountains all over the world.

'We're climbing all the way up there today?' he asked.

Tony laughed.

'No,' he said. 'But we'll see how far we can get by five o'clock then turn back. We'll do the whole thing at the first opportunity the weather gives us.'

Jack was glad he was fit. He didn't feel breathless like most of the others seemed to be. Even Daz was panting quite heavily. Jack and Kemal gradually drew ahead of the rest. After a while, the path became narrower and steeper, but Jack did not slow down. He whistled out of tune as he strode strongly higher and higher up the lower slopes of the mountain.

When he and Kemal reached a fork in the path, they stopped and sat on a rock to wait. Jack looked at his watch. Four-thirty. They would not be going much further today. By the time the others caught them up it would be time to turn back.

'I wish we could have started earlier,' he said. 'We would have been at the top hours ago.'

'Let's hope it's fine tomorrow,' said Kemal.

Jack breathed in the cool air and stared around him. On one side, he noticed that the land was quite flat to begin with. Then it rose quite steeply, the path zigzagging between jagged rocks. Beyond that, he could see the mountain towering into the now clear blue sky.

On the other side there was a very steep slope, not quite a sheer drop, covered in stones and rocks and small plants that clung to the shallow soil. He peered over the edge.

'A long way down,' Kemal said.

'Yeah,' said Jack. He turned back towards the mountain. 'But we want to go up, not down!'

A few minutes later, the others arrived. Jack and Kemal jumped up to greet them.

'Thought you must have got lost,' said Jack. 'We've been up the mountain and back while we were waiting.'

'Liar!' said Daz, dancing like a boxer in front of him.

Jack dodged about, imitating Daz, laughing. Then he leapt back.

'Hey! Careful!' shouted Mike.

But his warning was too late. As Jack's feet landed back on the ground he felt the loose stones shift beneath them and before he could do anything to stop himself, he was over the edge and beginning to slide down the hillside.

Chapter Three

At first, Jack felt excited, the kind of exhilaration you get when you're on the scariest ride in Alton Towers, but that only lasted for a few seconds as the fact flashed into his brain. He couldn't stop!

'Jack!' He could hear panic in Mike's voice.

'Stop mucking about!' Kemal was yelling.

'I'm not mucking about!' he wanted to shout, but there wasn't time. He was concentrating all his efforts on trying to stop.

'I'm sorry! I'm sorry!' Daz was screaming over and over again.

Jack was still on his feet, just, in a crouching position, trying to keep his balance. But at this rate, he would go on forever. If he sat down and dug his heels in, he thought he might stand a chance.

Sit down to stand a chance! Even in the hair-raising situation he was in, the joke flashed through his mind, but only for an instant. He bent his knees further and felt the hard ground jar against his body as his backside hit the hillside. He desperately forced his heels down, but he found that the loose stones gave him nothing to grip on. He realised that, instead of stopping or even slowing down, he was actually going faster.

'Help!' he screamed inside his head.

A feeling of panic cut through him like an ice-cold knife. He wasn't going to stop. He was going to fall all the way to the bottom. He was going to be killed!

'Grab that bush!' Mike yelled from above. His voice sounded much further away now, almost as if he was in another world.

But out of the corner of his eye, Jack saw a flash of dull green. There was a spindly, wind-blown bush, almost in his path. He reached out and snatched at it, but he winced in pain as the branches brushed through his hand and thorns ripped his fingers. He was travelling too fast! The bush was way above him already.

Then another bush appeared in his vision and he instinctively tried again. This time there were no thorns and he managed to hang on. For one moment, his hopes were raised. He had slowed down. The bush was going to save him.

'Yeah!' came a distant shout from Kemal. 'Hang on, Jack!'

Jack did hang on, for dear life, but just as he thought he might make it, the bush began to come away in his hand.

The roots could not hold his weight in the shallow soil and the bush leapt up into the air against the force of his efforts. The short pause in his fall was ended and the nightmare was beginning all over again.

Down and down he skidded and bumped, past several more bushes, which he tried to grab. Then, as he rushed lower and lower, the shingle on the surface was replaced by larger stones. The ground became rougher and Jack felt his body being bruised against rocks. He felt himself bounce over a boulder, but he could do nothing except lift his arms to protect his head.

His fall seemed endless and yet it was all happening so quickly. The voices from the path were still there, but Jack could not hear what they were trying to say. It was almost as if they didn't really exist, only in his brain. Everything was becoming a haze. He was no longer noticing what he was passing or where he was going. He was only conscious of how helpless he was and how much pain he was in. His hand hurt like mad where the thorns had ripped, his elbows were scuffed and scraped and his feet and legs were sore with his fight to stop himself. But they were nothing compared to the agony he experienced each time his body was bounced and dashed against the boulders.

I'm going to die! he thought.

A picture of himself scoring that final goal passed through his mind. *Goal!* Tears began streaming from his eyes.

I don't want to die!

Bounce, thud, bounce, thud... thud... thud...

'Aaahhh!' The pain across his back was excruciating. It felt as if he was breaking in two. He heard his own scream echoing around him, louder and louder and louder, never ending. 'Aaahhh!'

...Thud... Stop.

He lay there, still and silent, in a twisted heap. Pain shot through him, in black, ugly waves. He felt dizzy and sick. But he was alive.

He thought he could hear voices in the distance, but he was not sure whether he was imagining them. Where was he? How did he get here? He could not remember where he had come from or who he had been with. He was aware of his eyes misting over and he felt himself drifting away. Then there was nothing.

Suddenly, he was back on the football pitch, dribbling the ball, passing to Daz on his left. One, two, the ball bounced back to him off Daz's boot. One, two, deep breath, whack! Thwack! Goal!

Jack opened his eyes as consciousness returned, only to close them again as the pain took him over. His heart raced as he relived the fear of that dreadful fall. How long had he been lying here? It must be some time, he thought. He was feeling desperately cold. His teeth began to chatter and his body shook. He couldn't stop shivering.

He listened. There was total silence. Where was Daz? He knew he had been with Daz... and Kemal. Who else? His head swam again and he gave up trying to remember. He gritted his teeth. He just had to get through the pain. If only that would go away, he might be able to get up and look for help. But he couldn't move.

Jack was kicking a cushion across the room.

'Goal!' he yelled, leaping over the back of the sofa and knocking a pile of books onto the floor.

'Can't you think of anything else but football?' Emma was shouting at him. 'Can't you sit down for one moment and be quiet? Can't you let me have my own space for five seconds?'

Bleep, bleep, bleep. Craig sat gazing at his computer game. He didn't even notice that Jack was there.

He opened his eyes again. He seemed to be wedged tightly between two rocks. His right arm looked broken and both his legs were bent in an odd way. But the pain wasn't in his limbs. It was in his back. If only someone would come. He felt himself drifting away.

His mum was sitting with her feet up in the front room.

'Don't do anything foolish,' she was saying as a stupid kids' programme blared from the TV.

He woke again. His face felt numb, as if all the blood had drained away.

'Jack!'

Was that voice in his head, or was it real?

'Jack!'

The second time it was louder. It was real. Someone was there. He opened his mouth to call, but no sound would come.

'Jack! Are you there?'

He recognised the voice from somewhere. He tried again to call, but it was no use. His voice seemed to have dried up. Then he was aware of a movement about twenty metres above him to his left. Jack tried to focus, but his vision kept blurring. It was a man, he could tell by the voice, but who was it?

'Jack!' the man called. 'It's Mike.'

Mike. He remembered now. Flight-Lieutenant Mike Smith. ACT leader. Snowdonia. Walking up the mountain.

'Hang in there, lad!' called Mike. 'Help is on its way.'

He was lower now and Jack could see ropes. Mike must be abseiling down.

Jack saw himself up on a rock in the Lake District, standing with his back to the edge. He was slowly working his way backwards, letting out the ropes, daring himself to jump over and trust everything would hold. The rest was great fun and he reached the bottom too soon.

Suddenly, Mike was standing over him, his face very pale and his eyes staring. Jack felt tears trickling from his eyes.

'It's OK,' said Mike, very quietly as he crouched down beside Jack. 'They're sending the Mountain Rescue.'

Jack tried to answer and heard a deep groan that came from somewhere inside him. He couldn't stop shivering. Mike took off his jacket and laid it over him.

'Are you in a lot of pain?' asked Mike.

Jack managed a slight nod of the head. Then he blacked out once again.

They were in the ATC hut. Everyone was in full uniform. Flight-Lieutenant Smith was there, facing all the cadets and all the parents.

'I am very pleased to announce the winner of Cadet of the Year Award,' he said. 'And that goes to Jack Wallis.'

Mum and Dad were thumping him on the back.

Jack Wallis, Cadet of the Year! That was a bonus. It wasn't as if he had had to do anything difficult or horrible

for it. All those fantastic weekends doing all those exciting things.

He came to as a different sound broke the silence of the hillside. He frowned, trying to identify the sound.

Mike stood up and began waving frantically.

'Here it comes,' he said. 'It won't be long now.'

The sound grew louder and Jack recognised it. It was a helicopter. Of course, the Mountain Rescue. Above them, Jack could see an orange blur. The rhythm of the rotary blades confused him and made him feel sick again.

He didn't want to move from this place. It would make the pain worse. He didn't think he could stand that. If only he could curl up somewhere warm. If only they would leave him in peace to get over his fall.

The helicopter hovered overhead.

'They're winching someone down,' said Mike, crouching beside Jack. 'They'll have you out of here in no time and straight to hospital.'

Hospital? He didn't like the thought of going into hospital. That's where ill people went. His nan had died in one.

A long rectangular shape was floating down towards them, with a man attached to it. Soon the man was beside them.

'How bad is he?' the man asked quietly.

'Bad,' whispered Mike turning away, but Jack had heard him.

Bad? Jack didn't like the sound of that.

'It looks as if his right arm is broken,' said Mike, 'and both his legs. I can't tell about anything else.'

'You haven't moved him?' asked the man.

'No, of course not!'

The man crouched down beside Jack.

'Now then, young man,' he said. 'We're going to have to move you, but first I need to see where you've hurt yourself. It wouldn't do for me to make matters worse by shifting you wrongly, would it?'

He lifted Mike's coat and Jack felt gentle hands touching him, but even that increased the pain and he felt a swathe of darkness descending on him again.

Daz was dancing up and down like a boxer in front of him.

'Where's Jack?' he was yelling.

'I'm here!'

Jack began imitating Daz.

'Look out!' Mike shouted as Jack felt his feet slipping.

The next thing Jack knew, he was high in the air, being winched up into the helicopter. He felt very drowsy, but the pain had eased.

The man was beside him.

'I've given you a shot of painkiller,' he said as the stretcher was loaded on board.

Jack was already asleep as the helicopter swept over the mountain on its way to hospital.

Chapter Four

Jack stared at the white ceiling and wondered where he was. He was lying in a bed with white covers. Then he felt someone touching his hand and looked to one side. His mum was sitting there. Her eyes were red and her face was blotchy.

'…the disco,' Jack muttered.

'Disco?' said Mrs Wallis, jumping to her feet. 'What…? Oh, never mind… Nurse! He's awake!'

A young woman in uniform hurried towards them and stood on the opposite side of the bed.

A nurse? Jack thought. *So I must be in hospital. But why?* Then the pain in his back hit him and he winced. He noticed his right arm was in plaster. The bottom half of the bed was covered in a high arched frame. It was really odd.

'He said something about a disco,' said Mrs Wallis. 'Do you think he's delirious?'

'He's concussed,' said the nurse. 'Don't worry. It's quite normal for the mind to wander in and out of consciousness after such a shock to the system.'

'But is he going to be all right?'

'I'm sure he is, but it's very early days, Mrs Wallis,' answered the nurse. 'We'll just have to wait and see.'

They're talking about me as if I'm not here, thought Jack.

'I came as quickly as I could,' he heard his mum say in a tearful voice. 'My husband was working out on site and they couldn't get hold of him at first, but he's on his way now.'

'Good,' said the nurse. 'I wonder if he can hear us.' She bent towards Jack. 'Jack?' she said right into his face.

Jack looked into her deep brown eyes, but he said nothing.

'Jack?'

'He spoke just now,' said Mrs Wallis.

Jack stared back at the ceiling. He couldn't be bothered to speak. He felt too tired. The pain was getting to him.

Bright lights flashed all around him, red, blue, white, purple, yellow lights, round and round, on the ceiling in a brilliant pattern. It was dark between the flashes and very hot. Hundreds of people were squashed into the hall. They were all dancing.

A space was clearing round Jack as he danced. His friends had stopped to watch him. He spun, wiggled his hips, twisted and turned and leapt in the air.

'Fantastic!' screamed Lara against the loud beat.

'Jumping Jack Flash!' yelled Kemal.

'Show off!' yelled Daz.

Jack was laughing. He knew he was a bit of a show-off, but he didn't care. He loved disco dancing!

As Jack's eyes began to focus, he noticed that the colours of the disco lights had faded. Everywhere was white again. He seemed to be in a small room. There were several machines near him and he noticed a tube fixed to the back of his hand. He must be back in the hospital. It felt as if someone was drilling a hole in his body. He wondered how long before the pain would go away.

A man was standing there. He thought he knew him. Oh, yes. It was his dad. What was he doing here? Then Jack remembered hearing his mum say that dad was on his way.

'Hello,' said Mr Wallis. 'How do you feel?'

Jack was pleased that at last someone was actually bothering to talk to him, but he still did not have the energy to speak.

'We've all been worried,' said Mr Wallis, 'since we heard about your little tumble.'

Jack wanted to say that it hadn't been a little tumble, but a stinking great plunge down a mountainside, but he couldn't put the words together. He grunted instead.

Suddenly he was falling again. His hands reached out for something to save him. He heard Kemal's voice in the distance, 'Hang on, Jack!'

But he kept on falling and falling. His back was killing him.

'Help!' *he shouted inside his brain.* 'Let it stop, please let it stop!'

He found himself gripping the nurse's hand.

'All right?' she asked.

He groaned and she smiled down at him. Where was his dad? He could have sworn he was there a minute ago.

'I'll be looking after you while you're here,' said the nurse.

He groaned again.

'You don't have to speak if it tires you too much,' she said. 'It's enough to know that you're awake and know what's going on.'

But I don't *know what's going on,* he thought, *except that I'm in a hospital and that I've got a broken arm and a back that feels as if it's snapped in half.*

'The important thing is that you make a speedy recovery,' said the nurse. 'You've got loads of cards. Do you want me to show them to you?'

Slowly, Jack shook his head. He couldn't be bothered with them.

'All right,' said the nurse. 'When you're feeling better.'

He blinked and his mum and dad were sitting beside the bed. It was odd how people kept appearing and disappearing. Perhaps they weren't there at all. He couldn't tell what was real and what was in his imagination.

He was there again, being bashed on the rocks. Down and down, helpless, unable to stop the nightmare. He opened his mouth. He could hear himself screaming, screaming, screaming.

Everything was white, but he was still screaming. The nurse was bending over him with a worried expression on her face. His mum was crying. His dad was comforting her. He closed his mouth as he realised the scream had not been in his nightmare, but was for real. It seemed to echo round the hospital room.

'It's time for your painkiller,' said the nurse. 'I'll fetch it.' And she hurried away.

Later, when Jack woke from a more peaceful sleep, he saw his mum and dad sitting side by side near the bed.

'What's—?' he began huskily.

His parents leaned forward.

'What's going on?' Jack managed to ask.

'Well,' said Mr Wallis. 'You know about your fall, don't you? You're in a hospital quite near Snowdon. It's where the helicopter brought you.'

'You've broken your arm and both your legs,' said Mrs Wallis. 'But you've got some other nasty injuries. We don't know how serious they are. You'll have to have some tests when you're strong enough.'

'Tests?' Jack's mind shot to a classroom with lines of desks and everyone sweating over sheets of paper.

'On your back,' said Mr Wallis. 'You've hurt your spine.'

So that was why there was so much pain!

'You'll be in hospital for quite a while,' said Mr Wallis.

Good job it's the end of the season, Jack thought. *There'll be plenty of time to get fit before next season starts.*

'How long have I been here?' he asked.

'A couple of days.'

'*A couple of days?*' The effort of asking that question caused the pain to shoot through him again and he took some deep breaths until it had eased.

'You've been asleep most of the time,' said Mr Wallis. 'And you were in the operating theatre for several hours. They had to patch you up.'

'Loads of people have sent messages,' said Mrs Wallis, pointing to some cards on the bedside cupboard. 'Emma and Craig send their love.'

Jack looked at the cards. Who could have sent them? He wanted to know now. He watched his mum pick them up one by one and read the messages. They were from Kemal and Daz, from the ATC group, Emma, Craig, Aunty Jane, several neighbours and lots of friends from school.

'Several people rang, too,' said Mrs Wallis. 'Lara – is that that pretty girl who lives along the road? – and Daz's mum, some other school friends. Bad news travels fast, doesn't it?'

The next few days passed in a blur. Half the time, Jack could not decide whether he was in the real world or in his own head. His dad had to go back to work, promising to return at the weekend, but his mum stayed at the hospital and seemed to be in the room most of the time. Jack could do nothing, but lie still on his back and wait in a mixture of pain and boredom.

People kept appearing at his bedside. The nurse was there a lot and various doctors came from time to time, but sometimes there were different people, too. A physiotherapist came every day. Jack was thankful that the pain in his back wasn't quite so sharp now, more like a dull ache. His arm hurt, but it was strange how he couldn't feel his legs.

One afternoon, Mike arrived with Kemal and Daz. Jack's spirits lifted when he saw his mates walking towards him, but Kemal hardly said a word and Daz would not even look at him.

'How are you feeling?' asked Mike.

Jack grunted.

'We've come to the end of our week,' said Mike. 'We're off home tomorrow.'

I've missed it all, thought Jack, staring at the ceiling. *I wonder if they climbed the mountain.* He didn't have the energy to ask.

He was relieved when they left half an hour later.

'See yer!' said Daz as they walked away.

Jack was feeling utterly depressed. So his friends didn't need him while he was a virtual corpse. He hoped that was going to change as soon as he was out of this place.

At the weekend, his dad returned, as promised. As he strode into the room, Jack could see Emma and Craig behind him.

'Any better?' asked Mr Wallis. 'You certainly look less of a ghost!'

Jack nodded. He had had some tests and the nurse had been doing her best to keep him comfortable. Perhaps they would let him get up soon and then he would be allowed to go home.

Craig stepped forward and thrust something towards Jack.

'Here,' he said. 'I thought you might like this to help pass the time – when you're feeling well enough.'

It was Craig's Game Boy.

'But...' stuttered Jack.

'It's OK,' said Craig. 'I've got plenty of other things to do. Anyway, Mum says I spend too much time on this.'

'Thanks,' said Jack. He was amazed. When had his kid brother ever been known for his generosity?

But it was Emma who surprised him most. She elbowed her way past Craig and kissed Jack on the cheek. Normally, Jack would have shoved her off (not that she ever kissed him normally), but he felt strangely pleased. He could feel moisture on her face and realised his sister had been crying.

'Get well soon,' she whispered as she stepped back.

Suddenly, his heart began beating nineteen-to-the-dozen. What was going on? Why was everyone being so kind to him all of a sudden?

'What's up?' he said, alarm bells ringing in his head. 'Tell me. Why are you all behaving so strangely?'

Mrs Wallis gripped his hand.

'The doctor will be round shortly,' she said in an over-the-top cheerful voice.

'So?' asked Jack, a feeling like lead landing in his stomach.

'Well, she'll be bringing the results of your tests.'

For the next hour, Jack hardly heard a word of the conversation. Everyone seemed to be chattering too loudly or too fast about nothing in particular. They all seemed relieved when the doctor entered the room carrying several folders and files.

'I think maybe you two should wait outside,' said Mr Wallis. 'It's a bit crowded in here right now.'

Emma and Craig slid silently from the room. The doctor turned to Jack and he read a sad expression in her eyes. The lead weight inside grew heavier.

It was after they had looked at the X-rays and consulted the test results that the doctor took away the arched frame from the bed. Jack could just see along his body to his legs. The white plasters started below the knees and covered his feet. His toes stuck out like a row of pink sausages. He watched the doctor tickle his toes, but he felt nothing.

He stared disbelieving into her face. Was he getting the wrong message?

'Jack,' she said at last. 'You've broken your right arm and both your legs, but the main injury is to your back. You have severely damaged your spinal cord. This has caused paralysis in both your legs.'

Jack tried to sit up, but found it was impossible to move.

'It'll go away, won't it?' he asked, suddenly afraid.

'It looks as if you'll be getting round in a wheelchair from now on,' said the doctor.

'But how long before I'm walking again?'

The doctor shook her head.

'I'm sorry, Jack,' she said. 'I haven't explained myself very well. It's not quite as simple as that.'

'What do you mean?' cried Jack. 'Tell me. I want to know the truth.'

His pulse was drumming loudly in his head. He had the terrifying feeling that he knew what she was going to say.

'I'm sorry, Jack,' she said, 'but it may well mean that you'll never be able to walk again.'

Chapter Five

Jack stared. Was his hearing playing tricks? Was his brain totally mixed up? But his mum was crying again and his dad looked as if he had just lost a million pounds.

Jack frowned at the doctor.

'What...?' he whispered.

The doctor shook her head.

'I'm sorry,' she said again. 'I wish I could give you some better news, but I can't pretend. That wouldn't be fair on you. I had to tell you the truth.'

Jack lay stunned, trying to take it all in. Never walk again? That was impossible. They must have made a mistake. It wasn't Jack Wallis they were talking about. He's the super-sportsman, World Cup winner. They had the wrong one.

But all the signs pointed to it, didn't they? The fall, the pain, the sensation that his back had snapped in half, the tests, the X-rays, the fact that he couldn't feel his legs.

But she had used the word, 'never'. Never? That meant *never* being able to run again, or climb mountains, or dance at discos ... or ... play football.

'*No!*'

His yell came out like the cry of a wild animal and echoed round the room.

'*No!*' he screamed again. '*It's not true! It can't be true! Please, someone, tell me it's not true.*'

But no one spoke. He turned to his mum and dad.

'*Please!*'

They knew it was true. He could see it in their eyes. Maybe they had known for a while and hadn't dared tell him. Did Emma and Craig know? That would explain their strange behaviour. Did Kemal and Daz know? No wonder they couldn't face him and couldn't wait to get away.

The whole world knew. Jack Wallis, do you remember him? That ex-sportsman, ex-dancer, ex-footballer, *ex-person.*

The whiteness of the room became black. The entire world had gone black. He had dived into a deep dark tunnel where there were no lights, where there was no end. He felt his mum's hand gripping his in the darkness, but she could not pull him out. He was going to be left there forever, no good to anybody.

I might as well be dead. On the mountain, I thought I was going to die. I didn't want to die. Now, I wish I had.

He shut his eyes tight. He remembered doing that as a little boy, when something had frightened him. If he squeezed them really tight, the frightening thing would go away and when he opened them again, everything was all right. It wasn't going to work now, he realised that, but what else could he do?

'Jack.' His mum's quiet voice came from somewhere in the darkness. He turned his head away from the sound. He didn't want her pity.

He heard movement in the room. People were coming and going. He heard Emma's voice, whispering in the background. She must be really glad. She had her peace and quiet now he was out of the way.

Someone touched his arm.

'I'm sorry, Jack.' It was Emma. 'I said some horrible things to you.' She was crying again. 'I didn't want you to fall off a mountain. I didn't want this to happen.'

Do you think I did? he thought, but he kept his eyes screwed tight shut. He didn't want to talk about it, not with her, not with anyone.

Silence. They had all gone away. The room was empty. Good. He wanted to be alone.

He was back on the pitch. He felt the buzz and heard the crowd cheering him on. He heard Lara and Brook shrieking and saw himself tearing down the touchline with

45

Kemal and Daz right there with him. It was second nature to dodge round those defenders. It felt so good scoring that goal. He was sure it was only a matter of time before the England manager would be there, watching.

In a couple of years he could be signed on with one of the big clubs. It would mean lots of training and hard work, but it would be worth it. He was going to be the next Michael Owen!

Jack came down to earth with a thump. He was back in that dark tunnel. That daydream would never happen. The doctor's bombshell had told him that.

He heard the door click. He heard footsteps coming towards the bed.

'Jack? Are you awake?' It was the doctor.

Jack knew that he could easily pretend he was asleep, but maybe the doctor had come to say she had made a mistake. He turned his head and looked at her.

'I wondered if there was anything you wanted to ask,' she said.

So she wasn't going to admit she was wrong. He shook his head. He didn't want to talk to anybody. But then he changed his mind. Maybe he should know everything. He nodded and the doctor smiled.

'Good,' she said. 'I think it would be helpful to you if I told you more about your injury.'

He nodded again.

'I don't know how much you know about the spine,' she said, 'that it's made up of a long line of bones called vertebrae?'

'Yeah.'

'And that there is a spinal cord that runs from your brain, all the way through the centre of the vertebrae?'

'I suppose so.'

'And that if you damage that cord, you will have paralysis below where the damage is done?'

Jack said nothing.

'Well, I know this is painful to you in more ways than one, but you need to know what's happened to you. Do you agree?'

Jack shrugged his shoulders. He didn't want to hear it, but he supposed he would have to.

'The vertebra you've broken is in the middle of your back,' explained the doctor, holding out a sheet of paper. 'I've brought a picture of a skeleton to show you.'

Jack was back in the biology lab at school. They were learning about the human body. A picture of a skeleton stared back at him from the page of the text book. He glanced up at the biology teacher and sniggered.

'Cor,' he whispered to Kemal. 'It's the spitting image of him!'

The sniggers and giggles had spread along the row and then right round the class. It had ended up with the whole class getting into trouble.

Jack gulped and blinked back the tears that threatened at the back of his eyes.

He reached out his left hand and took the paper. The doctor pointed to a spot about half way down the backbone.

'This bone is known as T12,' she said. 'That's where the spinal cord is damaged. That's why the lower part of your body and your legs are paralysed.'

The repetition of those words made Jack's head spin. He dropped the paper and covered his face with his hand. The doctor kept quiet. He was glad. He didn't want her sympathy.

'What else?' he muttered after a while. 'You may as well tell me everything.'

'I'm afraid it has also affected your bladder and bowel,' she said. She spoke in such a matter-of-fact way that Jack didn't realise the significance of what she was saying at first.

Then it hit him. His mind spun into freefall. Another bombshell out of the blue! What did this mean? Was he going to have to wear nappies?

'You'll learn how to cope with that as you recover,' the doctor went on. 'There are various routines you'll get into. You'll manage very well, you'll see.'

Cope? Manage? At that moment, Jack didn't think he would be able to do either. It was getting worse and worse. What else was she going to throw at him?

After a while, he took his hand away from his face. The doctor was still there.

'I've got something else to tell you,' she said.

Jack felt sick. He steeled himself, ready for the next piece of devastation.

'We're moving you tomorrow – we've managed to get you a bed in a special hospital that deals with spinal injuries,' she said.

Jack felt a little of the tension draining away.

'You'll get the right kind of treatment there, more than we can offer you here. And the added bonus is, it's quite near your home. You'll be able to have lots of visitors.'

'If anyone bothers to visit,' Jack muttered.

'Oh, you'll get loads, you wait and see.'

I might not feel like seeing them, Jack thought.

'You'll travel by air ambulance,' said the doctor as she left the room. 'Good luck.'

The next morning, Jack was woken early by the nurse. She went through the daily routine of washing him. He hated it, although it wasn't quite so embarrassing now he was getting used to it, but he couldn't wait to be able to wash himself. Then she gave him his breakfast.

'Big day today,' she said. 'Lucky you, getting a helicopter ride!'

Jack didn't share her excitement. He had been in one helicopter already, not that he remembered much about it.

'It's a great hospital you're going to,' the nurse said. 'Marvellous reputation.'

'The doctor told me.' said Jack.

'You're lucky!'

Lucky? thought Jack. 'Why do people keep saying I'm lucky?' he said. 'What's so lucky about falling down a mountain and ending up paralysed?'

'Sorry,' said the nurse. 'Bad choice of word. I just meant...'

'It's OK,' said Jack. 'Forget it.'

As his bed was wheeled from the room an hour later, he had his first glimpse of the rest of the hospital. It seemed quite an old building. They passed along a narrow corridor and through a long ward with a row of beds on each side.

'All right, Jack?' called an old man from one of the beds. 'Good luck to you, boy!'

'God bless you!'

Jack raised his left hand.

'How do they know my name?' he asked.

'Oh, you're famous in here,' said the nurse cheerfully. 'They heard about your accident. They've been asking about your progress every day.'

Jack almost smiled. Fancy a bunch of decrepit old men asking after him!

It was the same all the way through the hospital. Men and women and even children waved and called out to him.

'Everyone wants you to do well,' said the nurse as they left the building and headed towards the waiting helicopter. 'And I'm sure you will.'

Chapter Six

As the helicopter buzzed across the country, Jack almost forgot about his injuries for the first time since the accident. He had a clear view of everything as they zoomed over fields and hills, motorways full of traffic, lakes and rivers. The ride was exhilarating.

But it ended too soon and Jack's spirits dropped as the helicopter swooped down and hovered over the pad in the grounds of a modern building.

'Welcome to our Spinal Injuries Unit,' said the porter who helped lift the stretcher from the helicopter onto a trolley, then pushed Jack into the building.

Jack didn't respond. He didn't really care where he was. Nothing was going to change what had happened to him.

But as soon as they entered the hospital, Jack could not help noticing the vast differences from the one he had just left. There were smaller airy wards with only a few beds in each. Most of the patients seemed quite young and a lot of them were lying flat on their backs like him or propped up in bed. There were also several people in wheelchairs.

Two nurses very gently transferred Jack on to a bed by a window. One of the nurses stayed beside his bed.

'My name's Andrew,' he said, 'and I'm your Named Nurse.'

Jack grunted. The pain in his back had grown worse and his right arm was throbbing. It must have been all the jolts of the journey.

'This only happened to you less than a week ago?' asked Andrew, looking in a file. 'It must have been terrifying.'

'Yeah,' said Jack. He looked at Andrew and guessed he couldn't be that many years older than him.

'One minute you're having a great time,' said Andrew. 'The next ... wham ... bang ... and here you are.'

'Yeah.' Jack couldn't think of anything else to say, but he thought Andrew was cool. He sounded sympathetic without overdoing it.

'You'll be up and about in no time,' said Andrew, 'as soon as your back's healed. You'll be the fastest wheelie in the west.'

'Maybe,' said Jack.

Jack thought the days would drag terribly, but he was wrong. There seemed so many things to do and because everything took six times longer than normal, he found he didn't have time to rest, to close his eyes and try to forget.

The first morning, they wouldn't leave him alone. He had visits from a counsellor, a physiotherapist and an occupational therapist, a teacher, a consultant and several student doctors. Andrew was around a lot of the time, too.

By the end of the day, Jack had learned how to feed and wash himself lying down and had heard more about his injuries and how they would affect his life. He had been prodded around in what Sarah, the physio, called "passive exercises" and had been shown stretching exercises for his arms. He had been given a couple of books by the Spinal Injuries Association. They explained everything about his injuries and how to live with them. Then he had been told about how he would be able to empty his bladder and bowel when he was up and about. The thought of having to do something like that filled him with horror, but Andrew assured him he would soon think nothing of it. His brain was reeling and he felt incredibly tired and depressed.

That evening, his mum and dad walked into the ward. His mum was carrying a bunch of grapes.

'This is a lovely place,' she said.

Jack frowned. Her voice sounded too bright as if she was trying to cheer him up. Well, she wasn't going to succeed. Nothing was going to make him feel any better. He watched her searching in his belongings. She found his cards and stood them up on his locker next to the bed. Then she sat down.

'How was the chopper ride?' asked Mr Wallis, helping himself to a grape.

His dad, too? He sounded like he was putting on an act.

'OK,' said Jack. *Better than the first time,* he thought, but he didn't have the energy to say it.

'We had a good journey home from Wales last night,' said Mrs Wallis.

'Roads weren't too bad,' said Mr Wallis. He held out two more cards. 'Shall I open these?'

Jack nodded.

'One from Lara,' said Mrs Wallis. 'Ooh, that's nice. And the other one's from Mr Oakley.' Her forced laugh jarred through Jack's head as she held the picture in front of him. He looked at the card, but didn't laugh.

'Emma and Craig send their love,' said Mr Wallis, eating another grape. 'Want one?'

Jack shook his head.

'The school phoned to ask how you are,' said Mrs Wallis.

'It only took us twenty minutes to get here today,' said Mr Wallis.

Jack wished they wouldn't rattle on like that. He wasn't interested. After a while, he closed his eyes and made out he was falling asleep.

'Poor boy, he's tired out,' said Mrs Wallis. 'Perhaps we'd better leave.'

Jack lifted his eyelids a fraction.

'Is there anything you'd like us to bring you?' asked Mrs Wallis.

Jack turned his head away. He looked at his cards on the cupboard when his parents had gone. He liked the one from Lara. Fancy her sending him one. To think that he might have asked her out one day.

'I'm living in a fantasy world,' he said out loud. 'She's not going to look twice at me now. What girl in her right mind is?'

'Don't knock yourself.' Andrew was walking towards him with a mug of tea. 'I bet she fancies you something rotten, whoever she is.'

'She might have done before,' said Jack, 'but not now.'

Andrew handed him the mug with a straw in it and helped him drink.

'Why don't you have a go at that Game Boy I noticed in your cupboard,' he said. 'You need something to help pass the time.'

'How can I? I'm flat on my back and I can only use my left hand. My right one's no good with this plaster right up to my fingers.'

'No problem!'

Andrew rigged up a table and propped the game in front of Jack.

'You'll soon get the hang of it,' he said.

Jack struggled for ages to keep the game still. If he gripped it with his left hand how could he use the thumb properly? How could he ever win?

His first attempt was useless. He had no control. Bleep, bleep, crash! The tiny man ran straight into an obstacle and was dead. He must be the fastest loser in history. Jack sighed. It was pointless! He might as well give up. He stared at the little screen and watched the man jumping up and down, waiting for his next attempt.

'Come on,' he seemed to be saying. 'Let's have another go.'

The second turn was nearly as bad as the first. Jack frowned and heard himself growl with frustration. He would have one more go, then he would give up.

At that moment, something clicked in his brain. No, he was not going to give up. Since when had he ever let anything beat him? He wasn't going to be defeated by a stupid game! He would play until he won. If only he could get his right thumb to work he might stand a chance. He adjusted the game, wedging it between the table and his chest. That was better. It was uncomfortable, but it gave him more control.

This time, he jumped one obstacle ... two ... three. He was almost up to the next level. Keep going ... bang! He was dead. That was three lives lost – not good enough. Anger flared up inside him. He gritted his teeth. Try again!

Concentrate ... over several obstacles ... up to the second level ... look out...! Missed! Great! He was getting there ... crash!

'Oh, you stupid...' he muttered to himself. 'Come on. Keep at it. Don't let it win! Get to the end... Win the prize!'

Two more attempts, further each time, getting there. He heard himself panting with the effort, felt his heart beating faster. His thumbs were dancing now ... nearly there ... up one more level ... past this obstacle ... yes ... yes ... yes!! Made it! Won the prize!

I knew I could do it!

He felt the glow of satisfaction on his face, but he was tired. That was enough for one night. He might play again tomorrow.

Jack woke next morning wondering why he wasn't feeling quite so miserable. Then he remembered his long battle with the game. He had won in the end. That's what was making him feel better this morning.

'That must be a great game.' Jack recognised the voice. It was a boy called Ben, from across the ward. Ben was fifteen. He had a disease that had been gradually damaging his spinal cord since he was five so he had no feeling in his arms or upper body, but had partial use of his legs.

'Yeah!' called Jack. 'I refused to let it beat me!'

'Good for you!' said Ben.

Time flashed by and although Jack found it impossible to accept that he was paralysed, he had moments when the black despair was fading a little. He guessed he must be getting used to the idea, ghastly though it was. He sometimes thought about his room at home, the posters on the walls, the general mess all over the floor. His mum had always been nagging him to tidy up. He missed it in this clean neat hospital. But how was he going to cope with going back there?

He spent a lot of time playing Craig's Game Boy or reading the books he had been given or doing the work set by the hospital teacher. He got to know Ben a little by calling across the ward. There was Josef, too, a very cheerful boy of ten whose spine had been broken right near the top, leaving him paralysed from the neck down. Jack couldn't understand how he could sound so happy.

Each day, Jack was put through physiotherapy exercises. He often talked to the occupational therapist and he had some visitors. Mike popped in a couple of times and Jack was really surprised when Mr Oakley ambled in one evening.

There was also another lady, who came in to talk to him several times. She explained that she was a counsellor, but

Jack didn't like her much. She reminded him of one of the teachers at school who couldn't keep control of the class. And her glasses annoyed him. And she kept asking him questions and trying to get him to talk about how he was feeling. And he wished she would go away. He clammed up. He believed her when she said she was there to help, but it didn't work. She didn't help him at all. He preferred Sarah, the physio.

His mum and dad came almost every day and sometimes Craig and Emma were with them, but Craig always seemed eager to get away while Emma spent her time bustling about around the bed. One evening she was worse than usual.

'Can I get you a drink?' or 'Let me tuck you in', or 'I'll just tidy your cupboard', or 'Here, have one of these grapes.'

Jack couldn't stand it, but he didn't have the energy to say anything. He supposed she was only trying to please him. It just happened to have had the opposite effect.

There were two things bugging Jack. He complained to Andrew about the first one.

'Nobody, not even my family, knows what to say to me,' he said. 'They all seem embarrassed.'

'They're probably trying not to upset you,' said Andrew.

Jack persuaded himself it didn't matter anyway. He didn't want to talk.

The second thing that bugged him, though, which upset him more than he liked to admit even to himself, was that there was no sign of Kemal or Daz – no message, no phone call, no visit. He had been cut off, just like that. Finito!

Still, what did he care? He didn't mention it to anyone. He could manage quite well without their so-called friendship.

Quite often, the team of doctors would pass through the ward. Jack got used to being prodded and poked and questioned.

'I'm very pleased with your progress,' said the consultant, one day. 'Your spine is healing very well. I think you're strong enough to sit up.'

'Good,' said Jack, feeling the slightest thrill of excitement in his stomach. 'I'm sick of looking at the ceiling.'

Ceilings were very boring things to look at. It would be great to be able to see things from a vertical position.

Later that day, Jack was being put through his exercises.

'We'll soon get those muscles toned up,' said Sarah.

Jack groaned. 'That won't make any difference,' he said.

He could do nothing about the tears that streamed down his face or the sobs that shook his body. Sarah sat silently beside him and held his hand. After a while, the sobs began to die away and he wiped his eyes with the back of his hand, but he felt so miserable.

'Sorry,' he muttered.

'Don't be sorry,' said Sarah. 'It's the most natural thing in the world. Of course you're devastated. Who wouldn't be?'

It made Jack feel a little better, to at least realise that no one would think badly of him for crying, for feeling this desperate.

'But you're young and fit,' said Sarah quietly, 'and you have to look after yourself. There's no reason why you can't get back to peak form.'

'What's the point?' Jack muttered.

'We need to work on your legs and lower body to keep the circulation going and stop all kinds of little problems that could occur. But the stronger we can make your arms and back, the better you'll feel about life and the more you'll be able to do.'

'Like what?'

'Well, I bet you were a sportsman, weren't you?' She put her head on one side. 'Let me guess. You were a footballer?'

Jack nodded, feeling the tears smart in his eyes again.

'A good one?'

'I was hoping to play for England,' Jack sniffed.

'Ah.' Sarah's voice was almost a whisper. Then she smiled. 'But we'll work very hard together and get you fit so you'll be able to choose which sport you take up. There's loads to choose from.'

'Such as?'

'Such as: basketball; cycling; swimming; skiing; table tennis – the list is endless. You never know, you could be Olympic Champion in a few years time. Think about it.'

Jack did think a lot about what Sarah had said when she had gone. His arm hurt and he still wasn't convinced that there was much point to getting fit, but she had sounded as if she really believed what she was saying. Maybe he should make the effort. Maybe he could take up one of those sports. But Olympic Champion? Fat chance!

Chapter Seven

Sitting up wasn't as straightforward as Jack had thought. For a start, he needed someone on each side to slowly lift his shoulders from the bed and a third person to raise the backrest behind him. Then there was the pain in the upper part of his back. And then there was the dizziness.

Jack found himself gripping the nurses' arms to try and stop the room going round and round. He felt seasick. He wanted to throw up. It was terrible! He closed his eyes to try to shut the sensation out, but it only made him feel worse. He was relieved when the backrest was lowered and his body became horizontal again. So much for looking forward to sitting up. He didn't want to do that again in a hurry.

But Sarah was encouraging.

'You did very well,' she said. 'That's quite normal for the first time. Next time will be better.'

Jack had difficulty believing that, but the second attempt was not so bad. He still felt dizzy, but he didn't feel so sick and he stayed vertical for ten minutes. He took a good look round the ward and saw his fellow patients clearly for the first time.

'I'm exhausted,' he admitted to Sarah after that second effort. 'How am I ever going to stay upright for longer than that?'

But the following evening, Jack was sitting up in bed when his parents arrived.

'Wow!' said Mr Wallis. 'You look fantastic!'

Jack gritted his teeth. He couldn't believe his dad could talk like that. What a load of old rot! He *didn't* look fantastic. There was no getting away from that. What did his dad know about it?

'Well done,' said Mr Wallis. 'That physio must work you hard.'

'Yes,' Jack muttered. 'She does.'

'What kind of things do you have to do?' asked Mrs Wallis.

Jack sighed. Then he told his mum and dad about his exercises.

'My, Jack,' said Mrs Wallis. She leaned forward and kissed his cheek. 'You've no idea how good it is to see you on the mend. We've been so worried. I've been missing you round the house, missing our little chats. It's been a bit quiet.'

Jack's temper boiled over.

'On the mend?' he said, anger burning in his throat. 'You've got no idea, have you? Missing our little chats? Is that all? You don't seem to realise what *I'm* going to miss! Like – everything!'

His mum was crying again, but Jack couldn't stop.

'How would you feel if it was you who was going to be stuck in a wheelchair for the rest of your life?' he demanded. 'Not able to do anything you want?'

'I'm sorry, Jack,' cried Mrs Wallis.

'The last thing we want to do is upset you,' said Mr Wallis.

Jack felt his anger dying away.

'Sorry,' he muttered. 'I didn't mean – only it's not fair!'

'We were only trying to encourage you,' said Mrs Wallis, wiping her eyes.

'Would it help to talk about it?' asked Mr Wallis.

'No,' said Jack.

He sighed again. If only he could get out of here and get back to his old life – and his old friends. Where were they just when he needed them most?

'Have you seen Daz or Kemal?' he managed to ask.

'No,' said Mrs Wallis. 'I can't understand it. I'd have thought they'd be up here all the time. They haven't even been round once to ask how you were.'

So his friends had deserted him, as he suspected. He shrugged off thoughts of them. Maybe he would understand their reasons one day.

But one evening, he was sitting up in bed reading when he was amazed to see Lara walking slowly towards him. She hadn't spotted him yet and was glancing nervously around her. He wished he could pull the curtains round his bed. He didn't think he could face her. Then it was too late. She had seen him.

'Hi,' she said shyly.

'Hi,' he mumbled.

'I've come to see how you are,' she said.

'Come to see what a freak I am?' he asked. He heard his voice sounding harsh and unpleasant.

'No.'

'What, then?'

'I...'

'Well, now you've seen me, you can go back and tell all your mates what a pathetic heap old Jack Wallis has become.'

'B-but...' Lara stuttered. 'Don't you want me to stay?'

Jack shook his head.

'If that's how you feel...'

Lara turned and walked away. Her shoulders were hunched and her head was down. Jack guessed she was crying. He cursed himself. What a stupid idiot! What did he have to go and do that for? He couldn't do anything right, could he?

Meanwhile, Maureen, the occupational therapist, had been finding things for him to do. She discovered that Jack had been interested in aircraft ever since joining ATC and had made several model aeroplanes, which hung from his ceiling at home.

'What kind of planes?' she asked.

'Mainly old World War II ones,' he said, 'a Lancaster bomber and a Hurricane, that kind of thing. My favourite's the Spitfire. I spent hours doing them.'

'Great. So now you're sitting up,' she said, 'you could make some more, couldn't you?'

'I suppose so.'

Jack didn't really feel like making model aeroplanes. He had loved making them before this had happened, but now, how could he love doing anything any more? How he wished he could wake up and find it had all been a horrible dream!

As time passed, Jack began to feel steadier. His balance was returning to normal and he could remain in a sitting position for longer and longer each day. It was much better to be upright at last. It was strange how the world had seemed so different from a horizontal outlook. He didn't feel so tired either, although the physio exercises grew harder all the time.

When he was strong enough, Sarah and Andrew helped lift him out of bed to sit in a chair. But when he realised how limp and helpless his legs had become, his depression returned. Everything had gone against him, just when he was on the brink of a glittering career on the football field. It wouldn't have been so bad if he had been an egg-head or a computer whiz, but no, it had to be a super-sportsman that went hurtling down the mountainside.

Why can't I be as I used to be? he thought. *It's so unfair! Why did this have to happen to me?*

'If only I hadn't gone to Snowdonia with ATC,' he muttered under his breath. 'If only we hadn't gone up that mountain, if only I hadn't started larking around with Daz...'

'I'd better help you get dressed,' said Andrew. 'You'll feel so much better with your clothes on.'

But Jack found it unbelievably difficult to even pull a sweater over his head and impossible to put on pants or socks or trousers. It made him feel so pathetic and useless, not better, as Andrew had predicted.

When he was dressed at last, Andrew fetched a big mirror.

'Right,' he said holding it up in front of Jack. 'Take a look at yourself.'

Jack had to admit, it almost looked like his old self, though this version was quite a lot thinner and paler.

'And another big day tomorrow,' said Andrew with a grin. 'You're getting your wheelchair.'

That hit home hard. It made everything more definite – and more depressing. A dull sick ache weighed in his chest.

A wheelchair – *his* wheelchair. This was it – the truth – Jack Wallis was going to be in a wheelchair for the rest of his life.

Jack hated it – being fitted for the right size and type of wheelchair – getting instructions in manoeuvring it around the ward. It made his arm and shoulders ache after only a few minutes and his hands became sore from pushing on the wheels.

'It's no good,' he complained. 'I'll never get used to this.'

'You're using muscles you've never had to use before,' said Sarah, kindly. 'This is why we need lots more exercises for your upper body and arms. Think of it as fitness training – that's what it is, after all.'

After a few days, Jack was just about managing to get about in his wheelchair. Sarah took him to the gym. It was an amazing place, full of machines of every kind you could ever imagine, for strengthening every part of the body.

'Wow!' he said, experiencing just a shadow of a buzz stirring inside him.

'Now the plasters are off your arm and your legs,' said Sarah, 'we can get down to some real fitness stuff.'

She showed him how various pieces of equipment worked then they looked at the weights. They watched other young people of various levels of disability working out. Jack exercised on one simple piece of apparatus for a few minutes.

'That's enough for one session,' said Sarah. 'Mustn't overdo it.'

Jack felt disappointed. Once he had started, he had imagined himself performing great feats of strength. Sarah laughed when she saw the expression on his face.

'If you could see yourself!' she said. 'You look like the cat whose bowl of cream has just been removed.'

'That's exactly how I feel!' said Jack and he couldn't help laughing with her.

'Do you know, you're a good-looking devil when you laugh!' teased Sarah. 'Pity I'm a good twenty-five years older than you!'

It was the first time Jack had laughed since his accident. He had forgotten what it was like. They left the gym with promises of a return each day.

The wheelchair wasn't so bad. It got him around. As the muscles in his arms developed and his hands became hardened to the stress of pushing the wheel, he began exploring the hospital, but he found it very difficult to be cheerful. He felt dull and uninspired. He watched others laughing and joking, but how could he join in?

He enjoyed his sessions with Sarah. She was the only one who could snap him out of it. Also he knew he was becoming fitter and his stamina was improving. Every day, he started with warm up exercises, followed by tone up on some of the machines and finishing with weight training. He became an expert at dressing himself and heaving himself out of bed. He even learned how to pull himself up off the floor and into his wheelchair.

Then one day, he noticed a boy of about his age, working on one of the basic machines in the gym. He was in a wheelchair, too, and he looked miserable.

He looks how I feel, thought Jack.

'Hi,' he said.

'Hi.' The boy didn't lift his head.

'I'm Jack,' said Jack.

'Eliot,' said the boy.

'How did you end up here?' asked Jack.

'Car accident,' said Eliot. 'What about you?'

'Fell down a mountain,' said Jack. 'Worse luck!'

'Yeah,' said Eliot.

Jack thought about Eliot when he was back in his ward. Maybe they could be friends. He needed new ones now his old ones had done the dirty on him. He was just thinking about Daz and Kemal when he saw Lara coming into the ward. He couldn't believe it! Was she willing to come and see him again – after how he spoke to her last time? He suddenly felt dead nervous. He didn't know what to say.

'Hi, are you feeling up to visitors today?' she asked

brightly as if nothing had happened before.

'I dunno,' he muttered, feeling his face heat up. 'What made you come back?'

Lara shrugged her shoulders.

'You were feeling bad last time,' she said. 'I was hoping...'

'Oh.'

'Did you get my card?' she asked.

'Yeah. Thanks.'

There was a long silence. Lara sat on the bed and swung her legs.

'What's—?' Jack began, but Lara had begun to speak at the same time.

'How's—?' Lara stopped too.

'Go on,' said Jack. 'You first.'

Lara shook her head and giggled. Then she delved in her bag.

'I brought you these,' she said, handing him a four-pack of cokes.

'Thanks,' he said. 'Want one?'

They both sipped at their cokes. Jack was glad of something to do while he tried to think what to say. It was dead weird. He wouldn't have been tongue-tied like this before.

'I've been psyching myself up to come,' said Lara.

'You didn't have to,' he muttered.

'No, I wanted to.'

'Why?' he asked. 'Curiosity?'

'No. I've been thinking about you – what it must be like...'

'So now you know.' Jack heard his voice as he said it. He sounded bitter and angry again. He looked at Lara and saw the expression in her eyes, a mixture of surprise and hurt. She stood up.

'If that's how you feel...'

'I ... I don't...' he said. 'I mean ... I'm sorry for what I said. It's just so hard to take it all in. I didn't think anyone would be interested in me now.'

'So you were wrong,' she said, sitting down again. 'I like you, Jack. You've always managed to make me laugh. Why does that have to change?'

She leaned over and kissed his cheek.

Jack couldn't help the smile that spread across his face. So Lara liked him. And she was still willing to come and see him, even though he had sent her packing last time, even though he was only half his previous self.

'Thanks,' he said. She couldn't guess in a million years how important her words had been. He swallowed hard and tried to act as if he hadn't just had a tonne weight lifted from his shoulders.

'Seen Daz or Kemal lately?' he asked in what he hoped was a casual voice.

'Course I have,' she laughed. 'Every day at school.'

'They OK?'

'Yeah.'

'It's just that I haven't seen them since a couple of days after – my – accident. They obviously don't want to know me now.'

'No, it's not like that...'

'Why haven't they been to see me then?'

'Well,' said Lara slowly. 'If you ask me, they feel guilty. I've heard them talking about it. Your fall knocked Daz for six. He says it was his fault. He was larking about and made you jump backwards. He can't face you.'

Jack nodded.

'Yeah,' he said. 'If Daz hadn't been such an idiot, dancing about like a boxer, I wouldn't have slipped.'

'He feels terrible about it.'

'Big deal,' said Jack, bitterly. 'That's nothing to how I feel.'

Lara put her hand on his arm.

'And Kemal somehow feels bad it wasn't him that fell,' she said, 'if you see what I mean.'

Jack was astounded. It was difficult to believe that these two hard nuts were so sensitive. He would never have guessed.

'Why don't you ring them,' said Lara. 'I'm sure they'd be glad to hear you're still in the land of the living, as it were.'

'I still think they should be the ones to make the effort to get in touch with me,' said Jack.

'But...'

Jack looked at Lara. She was very pretty and he liked her and she had made the effort to come, twice. He would do it for her.

'Oh, all right,' he said. 'I'll ring them later.'

'Great!' Lara stood up to go.

'Will you come and visit me again?' Jack asked.

'Do you want me to?'

'Yes.'

Jack was really pleased that she had bothered to come for the second time. Just that short visit had made the world of difference.

Chapter Eight

'Daz, is that you?' Jack heard himself croak strangely down the phone.

'Yeah, who wants to know?'

It was good to hear the old familiar voice. He coughed to clear his throat.

'It's Jack.'

'Jack! Wow! I recognise you now. What you doing? I mean, how are you? I mean—'

'All right.'

'Where are you?' asked Daz.

'At the hospital, where do you think?'

'I just thought you sounded near. I wondered if you were home – or – something.'

'No, not for ages yet, but the hospital's only about twenty miles from you,' said Jack. Why was Daz playing so dumb? 'And this is the twenty-first century, you know, modern technology and all that!'

'I … er … look…' said Daz. 'Sorry I haven't been to see you. I didn't know whether you'd want to see *me*…'

Jack didn't answer.

'Jack? Are you still there?'

'Yes.'

'I've been feeling—' Daz stopped. Jack heard him sniff then there was silence on the other end of the phone.

'It would be great to see you,' Jack said.

'OK,' said Daz. 'When?'

'Tomorrow?'

'OK. I'll come after school.'

'Great.'

Jack had wheeled himself to a lobby where there was a public phone. It was more private than the ward. He didn't want every pair of ears in the place listening in. It was hard enough making these calls as it was. He had had to force himself. He felt he was on some new robot-speak drive.

He picked up the receiver, pushed in the coins and dialled another number.

'Hello?' It was Kemal's mum.

'Is Kemal there please, Mrs Unel? It's Jack.'

'Jack? Jack Wallis? Oh, my poor dear. How are you? Kemal's been so worried.'

'Is he in? Could you fetch him, please?'

'Of course, dear.'

Jack heard her screeching excitedly up the stairs. In a few moments, he heard thundering footsteps then a panting voice.

'Hey, Jack.'

'I've just rung Daz,' said Jack, gabbling in his need to say it right. 'He's coming to the hospital tomorrow after school. Do you fancy coming as well?'

'Wow! Yeah. Great idea. Look, I'm sorry – my mum says I—'

'We can talk better tomorrow,' said Jack. He didn't want telephone apologies or confessions. He didn't actually want face-to-face apologies or confessions either, but after what Lara had told him, it sounded as if they needed to clear the air.

Jack had a restless night and was bad-tempered the next day. He realised he must be nervous. He couldn't wait to see his mates again and yet he was dreading it.

He was dressed in jogging bottoms, trainers and T-shirt and sitting in his wheelchair when Daz and Kemal breezed in. He watched them, trying to look cool, but he could tell they were as nervous as he was. He had decided he was going to get it all out in the open from the word go, but as they reached the bed he felt any confidence he had had draining away.

Daz handed him a chocolate bar and Kemal had a bag of fruit from his dad's greengrocer's shop, but it was like the last time he had seen them. Neither of them could look him in the eye and he could tell they were being careful not to look at his legs. And he couldn't stand the silence.

'So what's new with you two?' he asked. He tried to sound light-hearted although he was feeling anything but.

'Not a lot,' said Kemal, fumbling with his laces.

'How's school?' asked Jack.

'About the same,' said Daz glancing around the ward. 'Boring as usual.'

This was getting nowhere. Jack decided he would have to come straight out with it.

'I've been dead cheesed off that you didn't come and see me,' he said.

Kemal turned red and Daz gazed out of the window.

'Just because my legs are paralysed, it doesn't make me into some kind of freak,' he said.

They both stared at him. He pointed at his legs.

'They don't work, but the rest of me does,' he said. 'And I need my old buddies to be around, if they can stand me.'

Daz coughed nervously. 'We just…' he muttered.

'Well…' Kemal mumbled into his chest.

'Lara came to see me the other day,' said Jack.

'She never said,' said Daz, looking surprised.

'She told me you were both feeling bad about my accident,' said Jack.

'What's she been saying?' said Kemal.

Jack swallowed. How would they take what he was going to say next?

'She said you both felt guilty that I fell,' he said.

'Yeah,' mumbled Daz.

'I've had counselling,' Kemal confessed, looking as if he was about to cry.

'So have I,' said Jack. 'But I don't like mine much. My physio is much nicer. I can talk to her.'

'I was getting nightmares,' whispered Kemal.

'Nothing to what I was getting,' said Jack. Anger welled up in him. He turned to Daz. 'If you hadn't been clowning around—'

'I know,' said Daz. He hung his head.

'—I'd be keeping up my summer training. I'd be building up for the next season. I'd be able to...' He stopped and took a big breath. Why was he flaring up against Daz? It could so easily have been the other way round. It could have been Daz sitting here instead of him.

I'm so stupid. Anger surged into his head again. *It was my silly fault. I shouldn't have been such an idiot – typical Jack-in-a-box! – leaping about on the edge of a precipice.*

'It wasn't really your fault,' he said, punching Daz's shoulder then slapping Kemal's arm.

Daz rubbed his shoulder.

'Ouch!' he yelped. 'You been in training in the boxing ring?'

'Yeah,' said Jack.

After that, it was different. Jack showed them his skill with the wheelchair by taking them for a tour of the hospital. They told him all the gossip from school and what was happening in the neighbourhood. He told them about Ben and Josef and how he had met Eliot in the gym. He described his exercises and all the things he could never have dreamed anyone would have to do to make their bladder and bowels work. He realised that the more he told them, the better he was coping with it in his own mind.

He was relieved they didn't mention football. He didn't think he could face that subject yet. But he was glad he had asked them to come.

A few days later, after another visit from Lara and two more from Daz and Kemal, Sarah took him to the gym as usual. She pointed to two parallel bars about a metre from the floor. She helped him stand up between the bars, showing him how to support his weight with his arms.

'You must do this for a while every day now your legs are strong enough,' she said.

'Why?' Jack felt slightly dizzy.

'It's important you keep the blood circulating in your legs,' said Sarah.

'But my back...' Jack began. He was feeling tired already.

'Don't worry. Your bones have healed. As long as you have something to hold on to – a couple of chairs, perhaps

– you'll be fine. OK, that's long enough for today. We'll do it again tomorrow.'

When he returned to the ward, Maureen, the occupational therapist, was there waiting for him.

'We need to think about you going home,' she said.

Jack felt his stomach lurch. Part of him was dying to go home, but what would it be like for him in the outside world? Here, in the hospital, everything was designed for the patients; everything was laid on for them. He would have to fend for himself when he left.

'Don't panic. It could be a couple of months yet,' said Maureen. 'But we have to get everything ready. I've been chatting to your parents on the phone and we're going to discuss things in more detail when they come this evening.'

About seven o'clock, they all went to a small room off the side of the ward.

'When Jack comes home,' Maureen began, speaking to Jack's mum and dad, 'he'll need to be as independent as possible. Your house will have to be adapted.'

'We've already started that,' said Mr Wallis.

'Good,' said Maureen. She turned to Jack. 'Now this is you and the next phase of your life we're talking about. I want you to say exactly what you think. We all want to do the best for you.'

When his parents had left, Jack felt strangely detached from himself, as if he was looking down on the situation.

Was it *his* house that would have to be altered so much? He attempted to visualise himself in his new downstairs bedroom, which was the sitting room at the moment. Then he tried to picture the downstairs toilet being enlarged to include a specially designed shower. The doorways would be widened and there would be ramps put at both entrances. There were going to be so many changes. Maureen had thought of everything.

A week later, after Jack's physiotherapy session, including 10 minutes standing between the bars, Sarah surprised him.

'You're doing so well,' she said. 'We think you're ready for an outing. You're going home for a couple of hours.'

Jack gasped.

'Are you pleased?' asked Sarah.

'Yes and no. How am I going to get there?'

'We thought you might like to go out on to the main road and hitch a lift.'

Jack laughed. He really liked Sarah. She always got him into a good mood with her teasing.

'But whose car am I going in?'

'Your parents will be here in a few minutes.'

Jack had only just had time to put on his trainers when they turned up.

'Your carriage awaits,' said Mr Wallis.

Jack's mum wanted to push his chair, but he insisted on his independence and followed them to the car park. His dad stopped by a people carrier.

'Where's the old Renault?' asked Jack.

'Part exchange,' said Mr Wallis opening the boot and a rear door. 'We got quite a good deal. The Renault wouldn't have been big enough for all of us plus your chair.'

Jack wheeled to the side of the car, placed his hands under his thighs and lifted his legs then lowered his feet to the ground, pulled himself into an upright position, swivelled round and lowered himself backwards into the car. He only needed a little bit of help.

'Well done,' said Mrs Wallis. 'You looked as if you've done that thousands of times before.'

Jack grinned. Getting into the car had been a real achievement. It made him feel good.

They drove along country lanes, through villages and towards a town. Jack was enjoying himself. He felt he was looking at everything for the first time. He had been isolated from the outside world and had forgotten that three months had passed. It was now mid-summer.

After a while, he noticed some cyclists, then several joggers and a game of cricket. Then he saw some kids of about his age kicking a ball about in the car park.

Suddenly, he felt as if that football had hit him smack in the stomach. He was winded, sick and depressed. It had knocked him back into that dark tunnel. He would never be able to kick a ball like that again.

Never! It was such a hideous word. It was so final, a no-hopers' word. *Never!*

'It's not fair!' he muttered as he thrust his head down into his hands.

He barely took anything in after that. He didn't seem to realise he had to be helped out of the car and pushed into the house. He hardly tasted the cake Emma had baked for him or noticed that Craig chatted away the whole time he was there. He felt like an alien, visiting from another planet. He wanted to curl up somewhere and be left alone.

'Poor Jack,' said Mrs Wallis with a worried expression on her face. 'We wanted to make you feel good about coming home.'

Jack said nothing. He could not even force a smile. He was relieved when his dad said it was time to go back. He kept his eyes shut all the way in the car.

'Did you have a good time?' Sarah asked brightly the next morning.

Jack shook his head.

'What's the matter?' she asked, putting her hand on his shoulder.

'I saw a crowd of boys playing football,' Jack mumbled under his breath. 'It suddenly hit me. I won't ever play again. That's all.'

'Don't say "that's all",' Sarah said quietly. 'It's a big thing for you. But, like I said before, it's time we found some sport that you *can* do.'

Chapter Nine

Jack had not realised how many sports facilities there were at the hospital or within a few miles. During the next week, he tried out several sports, but he soon discovered that some of them were not for him. He was no good at archery. He missed the target by miles and almost fell out of his wheelchair. Swimming was very difficult because he had always relied on a strong leg kick. He ached all over after that. Table tennis was boring and he had never liked snooker.

He watched videos of disabled people horse riding, playing tennis, golf, rugby and many other activities, but he wasn't interested in any of those.

'How about basketball?' said Sarah.

'All right,' said Jack. He had been a good player before his fall. Maybe it was possible.

Immediately, Jack began to enjoy himself. He had developed strong shoulder muscles and good balance and he could move his wheelchair with skill. It was tricky throwing and catching and bouncing the ball at the same time, but he felt the old buzz of excitement returning and he was soon aiming at the basket.

Goal!

That word hit his brain like an explosion. He felt light-headed. He clutched the arms of the chair to steady himself. He grinned. He might not have the legs, but he could still score baskets. Brilliant! Maybe this would be his sport from now on.

But that evening, while his mum was visiting, Jack turned the TV on for the athletics, one of his favourites. He had been a fast 100-metre sprinter, but he liked to think of himself as an all-rounder. This evening's programme was highlighting disabled people in athletics.

The longer he watched the programme, the more interested he became, until suddenly he saw something mind-blowing. It was the women's wheelchair 400 metre race. He watched the technique of the competitors and the determination on their faces. He was totally impressed by one quite small young woman called Tanni.

'Come on!' he yelled as she drew ahead of the rest. 'Yeah, come on. Keep going. You can do it!'

Andrew hurried over.

'What's all the shouting about?' he asked.

Jack pointed at the TV.

'That's what I want to do,' he said. 'There's an athletics track near here. I want to join. I'll train hard, like Sarah said, and maybe one day...'

'That's the first time I've heard you sound like our old Jack,' said Mrs Wallis with a smile.

Jack smiled back. He was pleased to admit he had begun to feel more like the old Jack, too.

The following week, Sarah took Jack and his dad and Eliot to the athletics stadium. It was fantastic. Everything was built with disabled sportsmen and women in mind. Jack couldn't wait to go through on to the track.

He closed his eyes and let his imagination take over. The roar of the crowd was in his ears. The atmosphere was electric. It was the final of the 400 metres. His eyes opened and he entered the arena.

He was in Lane 5. Eliot was in Lane 3. Jack looked up at the stands, took in some deep breaths then focussed his eyes on the way ahead. His mouth was dry and his heart was pumping fast.

He heard the starter's gun in his head and thrust at the side wheels with his hands. Round the first bend, he could hear Eliot breathing heavily. Half way round, he knew that Eliot had dropped out. He was on his own. His arms ached, his back was hurting and he felt exhausted, but he was determined to keep going. He had a real struggle, but he made it all the way round. His dad was waiting by the side of the track.

'You'd really like to do this?' he asked.

Jack nodded. He hadn't been so sure of anything for ages, not since his accident. One day. There wasn't any harm in ambition, was there? Eliot trundled slowly over to join them.

'I'm not as fit as you,' he said.

'We could train together,' said Jack.

Eliot proved more of a competitor than Jack had realised. As they trained in the gym and on the track over the next few weeks, he noticed Eliot's muscles strengthening and his times for the 400 metres gradually improving. It gave Jack a new challenge – to always keep ahead. His own training was going very well. It wouldn't be too long before he was ready for his first race.

More and more, he was thinking about going home. He still had mixed feelings about it and his confidence failed each time he wondered how he would manage. Then he and Eliot went to talk to Josef. Although Josef was almost totally paralysed, he was always positive and cheerful.

'I'll be ready to go home soon,' Josef said. 'I'm really looking forward to it. I'm going to learn to ride a horse and we're off to Disneyland next year. What about you? What are you going to do when you get home?'

Jack was amazed that Josef could think like that. 'Well, I'm in training on the athletics track,' he said. 'That will keep me busy.'

Seeing Josef's horrific injuries made Jack realise that he wasn't so badly off after all. He was glad he had got to know him, and Eliot, of course.

'Let's swap phone numbers,' said Eliot the day before Jack was due to leave. 'Then we can text each other when you're at home and meet up later.'

Jack was pleased. Having new friends with similar problems would be great.

Maureen had set everything up for going home.

'The alterations are finished,' she told him.

Jack already knew. His parents had been keeping him up-to-date.

'I think I'm ready to go home,' he said. 'But I'm dead nervous.'

'Of course you are,' said Maureen. 'But you'll be fine.'

Sarah had been preparing a strict regime of exercises for him to continue.

'It's very important that you stick to these,' she said. 'And you must remember to stand up for a while each day. And don't forget to keep an eye on your skin. You don't want any pressure sores to build up on your bottom!'

Jack grinned. 'Yes, ma'am, no, ma'am,' he said. He was going to miss Sarah. She was so lively and positive and always made him feel it was worth the effort.

'When you come back in for your check-ups,' she teased, 'I shall expect to find a handsome young man honed to perfection!'

'Pity you're a good twenty-five years older than me!' Jack said, remembering her words.

'Ooh! Now we see the true cheeky side of Jack, the lad! You'll go far!' She laughed. 'You're going to succeed in a big way. I have trust in you, Jack. I know you can do it.'

Jack had imagined that going home would be the same as last time, but he was shocked to see a crowd on the pavement outside his house and a giant banner saying 'WELCOME HOME, JACK!' stretched across the front of the house. A cheer went up as he self-consciously heaved himself out of the car into the wheelchair and he forced himself to grin and wave, though he felt like crying. His brother and sister were waiting at the front door. Emma raced out to meet him and began to push his chair towards the house.

'Let me,' he muttered as they trundled up the ramp. 'I don't want them to think I'm a complete zombie.'

But Emma ignored him and there was nothing Jack could do until they were inside.

'You could have allowed me to push myself,' he grumbled as soon as the door was closed.

Jack soon forgot his annoyance as he entered what used to be the sitting room. He was stunned. All his stuff had been moved downstairs, his aeroplanes hung from the ceiling and his posters had been blue-tacked up on the wall.

'Well?' asked Mrs Wallis. 'What do you think?'

'It's...' Jack couldn't put it into words. It was *his* bed, *his* junk, but it didn't feel like *his* room.

'Emma and Craig did it,' said Mrs Wallis.

Jack tried to smile. His brother and sister obviously had taken a lot of care over it.

'Thanks,' he said.

'Got to do something at the weekends,' said Craig. 'There's absolutely nothing on TV.'

Jack whipped round and stared at his brother.

'Only joking!' said Craig.

'But you haven't seen the half of it,' said Emma, grabbing at the wheelchair and propelling Jack towards the back of the house. 'Come on. I'll show you.'

The whole house had changed. As well as the enormous new shower room, there was a big extension on the back of the kitchen. It was all rather overwhelming. He realised it had been done for him, but it wasn't home as he had remembered it.

'How did all this get done so quickly?' he asked. 'I didn't notice it when I was here before.'

'It was started by then,' said Mr Wallis, 'but you had enough on your mind that day.'

Jack wheeled himself into his new room and shut the door. He needed to be on his own, to think. He took in some deep breaths and closed his eyes. It was hard to take everything in. He had grown used to the staff and patients and all the routines of the hospital. Now he was going to have to make the most out of his new situation.

The door opened behind him.

'Can I get you anything?' Emma asked.

'No, thanks.'

'A drink? We bought some of your favourite—'

'I'm all right, thanks.'

'Something to eat?'

'Emma!' Jack could feel his hackles rising. She was fussing again. 'No!'

But she started again as they sat down for their evening meal. She was being so *nice* to him!

'Are you comfortable?' she asked after she had held his arm as he lifted himself on to a chair. 'Shall I fetch you a cushion?'

'No, I'm fine.'

'I'll get you a coke, shall I?'

'OK.'

'We thought you'd like pizza, your favourite,' she said.

'Thanks.' He had gone off pizza, but he didn't say anything. He knew she meant well even though she was getting on his nerves.

Craig was unbelievable, too. Non-stop chat!

'Hey! You'll never guess!' he began. 'I sorted out Mr Barney's computer – he'd lost some important files – I found them.'

'Boring!' sighed Emma.

'I can't help being a genius, can I?' Craig said.

'Stop boasting.'

'I'm not. They can't find anything difficult enough for me at school. I'm the biggest window in Windows!'

'And the biggest mouth!'

'They can't cope with me.'

'I'm not surprised. You're such a pain in the butt!'

'No buts,' laughed Craig. 'It's a certainty! I'm top dog!'

He went on like this all through the meal, joking and laughing and cheeking their mum and dad. Where was the quiet boy of a few months ago?

Jack didn't speak. He couldn't keep up with them. He had been away so long he didn't seem to fit in anymore. He decided he would try and keep out of their way as much as possible. He shut himself in his room and rang Daz.

'I'm home,' he announced. 'You should see the changes they've made here. I hardly recognise the place.

And to make things worse, my sister's become my nursemaid and my brother's become the loud-mouth of the year!'

'Instead of you?' said Daz with a chuckle.

Jack thought about that when he had rung off. Was Daz hinting that he was jealous of Craig?

One thing he was certain of: being home wasn't going to be easy.

Chapter Ten

The following morning, Jack decided he wanted to make another model plane. The one he had made in hospital had joined the others, but there was still a lot of room on the ceiling.

'I'll take you downtown in the car after lunch,' said Mrs Wallis.

'No,' said Jack. 'I want to see if I can do it in my wheelchair.'

His mum looked doubtful, then nodded.

'All right,' she said. 'I'll come with you.'

'I'll be all right on my own,' said Jack. 'I am fourteen.'

'Just for the first time,' said Mrs Wallis. 'To make sure there are good slopes for crossing the roads.'

Jack was glad she had insisted on coming, though he didn't admit it. He didn't want to get halfway there and find he was stuck. That afternoon, they came across only one problem where a car had parked across a slope near a corner. Otherwise he managed everything on his own.

They chatted all the way to the town and he told her about Eliot's suggestion that they keep in touch.

'And I want to join the sports club,' he said.

'Good idea,' said Mrs Wallis. 'Oh, look, there's Sandra.'

Jack saw his mum's friend hurrying towards them.

'Hello,' she said to his mum. 'I've been meaning to get in touch about Wednesday's meeting...'

She rattled on for several minutes then shot off along the road.

'Well!' said Mrs Wallis, her eyes angrily watching Sandra rushing away. 'She could have spoken to you.'

'I might as well be invisible,' said Jack.

'Some people!' said Mrs Wallis. 'How rude and inconsiderate can you get? I'm sorry, Jack.'

'I'll have to wear a sign,' he said, bitterly. 'This boy is a human being. Please talk to him.'

He had been looking forward to coming into town, but he wasn't enjoying it anymore.

'Let's go and buy your model,' said Mrs Wallis.

They hurried to Brown's Hobby Shop and pushed open the door. But there was a step and Jack needed help. Once inside, he scoured the shelves for aeroplane kits. At last, Mr Brown asked his mum what they were looking for.

'My son's the one you need to ask,' said Mrs Wallis.

Mr Brown looked down at Jack.

'Well, sonny?' he asked. 'How can I help you?'

Jack seethed. He was fourteen and not this man's sonny and he had been in this shop dozens of times and never been spoken to like that before. He managed to swallow his annoyance and ask about the kits.

'We've got plenty,' said Mr Brown. 'They're upstairs – oh!'

'They used to be there,' said Jack, pointing to a shelf in the shop.

Mr Brown looked at Jack over his glasses.

'I remember you now,' he said. 'You bought a Hurricane and a Spitfire. What have you been doing to yourself?'

Jack felt his confidence growing as he told Mr Brown about his fall and his stay in hospital. It was the first time he had actually talked about it to a comparative stranger. Then he chose a kit from the ones that Mr Brown fetched downstairs.

'I'll bring the others down,' said Mr Brown as they were leaving.

Emma began fussing again from the moment they came in the front door. She brought him a drink that he didn't want and fetched him a book from his room when he mentioned he was going to read it. Jack bit his lip. She was only trying to help. But it was the final straw when Emma began to smooth down his windblown hair.

'Don't fuss!' he snapped. 'You're like an old mother hen.'

'What do you mean?' Emma snapped back.

'You've been treating me like a baby ever since this happened,' he said. 'All I want is to live as normally as possible. I don't want fussing over, just a bit of understanding. Please leave me alone.'

'Well, of all the ungrateful, spoilt brats!' she exclaimed. 'After all I've done for you.'

'I'm not ungrateful.'

'Yes you are,' she went on. 'Having everything your own way—'

'You call this—' he said.

'—and getting all the attention. Mum and Dad have talked about nothing else for the last months.'

'Well, look at me. How would you like to be like this?'

'Stop feeling sorry for yourself.'

'I'm not!'

'You are!' Emma burst into tears.

At that moment, the back door opened and Mr Wallis walked in. He grinned, put his hands over his ears then threw back his head and roared with laughter. Jack and Emma stopped mid-row and stared at their dad.

'What's up with you?' demanded Emma, wiping her eyes.

'I could hear you halfway down the road,' choked Mr Wallis. 'I thought, "That sounds just like old times."'

Jack and Emma weren't speaking for the rest of the day. They glared at each other over the evening meal then Jack went to his room. He decided to text Eliot.

`Hi,` he typed. `I'm home. How's things?`

He was chuffed when a message came back a few minutes later.

`Hi, guess what?` it said. `Really excited. Going home soon!`

`Great! Don't go for a few days,` Jack typed. `Coming to hospital for check up next week.`

`See you then,` came the reply.

He felt more relaxed. Texting Eliot had taken his mind off all the things that had been getting to him. He was looking forward to seeing Eliot again, especially when they got back together for training. He was just putting a CD in his stereo when the doorbell rang. He heard his mum open the door.

'Hello. Is Jack around?'

Jack recognised Daz's voice. A warm feeling spread through him. The fact that Daz had come to see him now he was home proved he hadn't been deserted.

'He's in his room,' said Mrs Wallis. '—no, not up there, in here.'

There was a light tap, then the door swung open and Daz appeared, followed closely by Kemal. Kemal stared around him.

'Wow!' he said. 'This was your front room.'

'Yeah,' said Jack. 'And now it's my bedroom.'

'It's cool,' said Daz.

They both looked slightly embarrassed as they lumbered over to Jack's bed and sat down. Jack tensed up.

'What's up?' he asked. Surely they didn't have a problem facing him again?

Kemal and Daz looked at each other then at him.

'Well—' said Daz.

'—we wondered whether to ask you—' said Kemal.

'—you see, we're going to the match tomorrow—'

'—and we wondered if you might like to come?'

The match! That meant only one thing – football – the new season was well under way. He had thought he would be fit to play. He understood why they had found it hard to ask him. Could he face it?

He felt a slight dizziness as memories of playing came flooding back into his head. He really had to get rid of the ghost of football. But it wasn't that simple. Going to watch a game might be just the thing to help him manage it. Or would it?

'Can I think about it?' he said.

Jack turned on the CD player and his favourite rock band blasted out across the room. He tried to blank out everything, but the question kept leaping up at him.

'Can I face it?'

The track finished and there was silence for a few seconds. Daz and Kemal were watching him. He was pleased they had asked him and they looked as if they genuinely wanted him to go. He swallowed hard.

'Yeah!' he said, hoping he wouldn't regret it. 'I'll come.'

He could see Daz and Kemal relax, but suddenly, Jack gasped.

'Oh, no!' he cried. 'Of course I can't go. Not like this.'

'Don't worry,' said Daz with a grin. 'We've thought of that. It's all arranged. We rang the ground and worked on them a bit. You, me and him, we all get to go in the special enclosure.'

Jack couldn't help laughing. 'So that's why you asked me!' he said. 'So you'd get the best seats in the stadium!'

'No, honest!' said Kemal.

'You lot? Honest?' said Jack. 'In another world, maybe!'

'Jack!' protested Kemal.

'How do we get there?' demanded Jack. 'I bet you haven't thought of that.'

'Yes we have,' said Daz. 'We've arranged it. Your dad's taking us.'

'Crafty lot, doing all that behind my back,' said Jack, but he was secretly pleased that they had taken the trouble. He hoped he wouldn't regret agreeing to go. He had a whole day to worry about it.

They arrived at the ground in plenty of time. As they made their way towards the special enclosure, Jack felt pleased with himself. He was coping so far. He hoped he was going to have a great afternoon. He was impressed with the stadium, too. A lot of alterations had been made since he was last there and the facilities seemed excellent. And the best of it was, they had a brilliant view over the pitch.

After a while, he noticed a few people staring at him.

'What do they think they're looking at?' he said, annoyed. 'Never seen someone in a wheelchair before?'

But then the teams ran out. The crowd roared and the atmosphere in the stadium was like a blast of electricity. It overwhelmed him. He wanted to burst into tears. He put his hands over his face and took some deep breaths.

'You OK?' Daz asked.

Jack said nothing. He wasn't sure. He hoped he wouldn't make an idiot of himself in front of his mates. He needed to take a grip of himself. He thought of what Sarah had said. It was time to concentrate on something else. The trouble was it was one thing saying that, but another thing for it to happen. He was enjoying the training and he was looking forward to racing, but – football – it had been his life.

He lowered his hands and looked down at the pitch.

'Yeah,' he said, gripping the wheels of his chair. 'I'm OK.'

It was a great match. Their team won 3-2. A mixture of emotions swept through him as the game went on. One minute he felt like crying, the next he was boiling over with excitement. Gradually he found himself becoming more and more involved and in the end he was shouting and cheering and booing with the crowd. When the winning goal was scored, he grabbed Kemal and Daz and hugged them.

'No kisses!' said Daz.

Jack laughed. That was his line, but he didn't mind Daz using it.

After all the excitement of the match, Jack suddenly felt tearful again. He hoped Daz and Kemal wouldn't notice. If they did, they certainly didn't say anything and Jack was thankful for that. They waited until the crowds had gone before making their way down to the exit where Mr Wallis was waiting. They were laughing as they came up to the car. Jack grinned at his dad.

'I think that's done you a power of good,' said Mr Wallis.

Jack nodded. He thought it probably had.

The next morning, Emma was in the kitchen when he came in for breakfast. She made herself a cup of tea and sat down at the table.

'You could have asked me if I wanted one,' said Jack.

'You told me you wanted me to leave you alone,' said Emma.

Jack sighed. She didn't have to take him quite so literally.

'So what's that sigh meant to mean?' asked Emma.

'You just don't understand, do you?'

'No. You're dead right,' she snapped. 'I've never been able to understand you. First of all, you're a right pain in the buttocks and won't leave me alone when I'm trying to study, then you worry us all sick by trying to kill yourself.'

'I did no such thing!' Jack shouted. 'It was an accident—'

'—and then, when I try and make an effort—'

'I don't want you to put yourself out for me.'

'I won't, don't you worry. And now you come lording it around here,' Emma went on, red in the face and very angry. 'You don't realise how it's been for us. I had to do all my exams while you were at death's door. I saw nothing of Mum or Dad. Craig and I had to—'

'Well, I'm sorry,' yelled Jack. He hoped he sounded extremely sarcastic. 'I'll make sure I don't do anything else that might get in your way.'

Emma got up and rushed out of the kitchen, slamming the door behind her. Jack made himself a cup of tea and some toast. He was furious with Emma. How would she like it? But the longer he sat there, the more he began to feel guilty. Perhaps Emma and Craig had had to put up with a lot over the last five months or so. And he had forgotten all about Emma's exams. He knew how important they were to her, even though he had tormented her before the trip to Wales. He wondered how well she had done.

Ten minutes later, Emma crashed back into the kitchen. She marched to the sink and thumped her cup hard onto the draining board.

'Emma.'

'What?' Her voice was still harsh and angry.

'I'm sorry.'

'What do you mean? Sorry for what?'

Jack suddenly felt his eyes fill with tears. What was the matter with him? His emotions were always upside down. He turned away. He didn't want his sister to think he was a wimp. But she had noticed.

'You can't just turn on the waterworks every time you want sympathy,' she said, though her voice was quieter.

'I'm not,' he sniffed. 'I don't want sympathy.'

'Well, it jolly well looks like that to me,' she said.

'Look,' he said, brushing away the tears and turning back. 'Can't we have a bit of a truce? I know I used to make your life hell and I'm sorry, but I can't help what happened to me. I can't help it if Mum and Dad abandoned you. They'd have done exactly the same if it had been you that fell down the mountain.'

'I suppose so,' Emma muttered, sitting down at the table. 'But when I tried to look after you, you—'

'But that's what I'm trying to explain,' said Jack. 'It's not that I'm ungrateful and sometimes I'm going to need your help, but I've got to become independent. They stressed that at the hospital. I've got to get used to the fact that I'm like this for life and it's not easy, I can tell you.'

'I can see that,' said Emma. 'OK, pax.' She held out her little finger. Jack stared at her. They hadn't done that since they were kids. Then he smiled and linked his little finger with hers and they shook.

'We're bound to have a few bust-ups,' said Emma. 'Life wouldn't be normal if we didn't, but we'll both try.'

Jack nodded.

'How did your exams go?' he asked.

Emma's face suddenly creased up as if she was going to cry. Jack felt bad. It was his fault. If only he had left her alone when she was revising.

But Emma wasn't crying, she was laughing.

'Five A's, two B's and two C's!' she said. 'I couldn't believe it!'

'Brainbox!' Jack said, but the relief he felt was very strong. It looked as if he hadn't ruined her entire life.

'Next time, Jack,' said Emma, giving him a hug, 'you can disturb me as much as you like.'

Chapter Eleven

The welcome Jack received at the hospital was amazing.
Lots of people that he hardly knew greeted him like an old
friend. As he entered the physiotherapy department, Eliot
zoomed towards him in his wheelchair.

'Hey!' he said with a beaming smile. 'I've missed you.'

'Thanks,' said Jack. He was pleased. It looked like they
were going to be great friends in the future.

'What's it like, going home?' asked Eliot.

'Great!' said Jack. Then he pulled a face, 'some of the
time. But not easy.'

'How do you mean?'

'Oh, you know, you can't always go where you want,
like upstairs in buildings and you wouldn't believe how
some people treat you.'

'How?'

'Sometimes you might as well not be there,' said Jack.
'Some people talk over you or treat you like a half-wit or a
kid of two. It's really depressing, but most of it's ok.'

At that moment, Sarah breezed in.

'Hi, gorgeous!' she said. 'Wow! You're looking altogether different already. Going home certainly suits you! But have you been keeping up your exercises?'

'Yes, ma'am,' said Jack.

'See you later,' said Eliot as he left them. 'Have fun!'

'What, with Sarah?' called Jack. 'The slave driver of the year?'

He pinched himself to make sure he was not in one of his daydreams. It had felt just like his old self, saying that. He remembered how he used to cheek Mr Oakley.

Sarah grinned.

'Double trouble for you, my lad!' she said.

The exercises went well and although Sarah did pile them on, he found he was enjoying himself and built up a good sweat.

'Been to the athletics club yet?' Sarah asked.

'Give us a chance!' Jack puffed. 'I haven't had a minute. But it's the next thing on the list.'

He sat straight and flexed his biceps. They were a lot bigger than the pimples they were before. At this rate he would soon be ready to compete.

'I'm impressed!' said Sarah.

He smiled. As usual, she made him feel good, so he was in a positive mood when he reached home. He sent a text message to Eliot straight away.

`Great to see you. Good luck going home.`
Eliot answered immediately.
`Ta. I'll let you know how I get on.`
`Sarah put me thru it today,` Jack wrote.
`She told me. Ha, ha.`
`Going to athletics club tomorrow,` Jack sent.
`See you there as soon as I'm fit,` Eliot
sent back. `Can't wait.`

Jack couldn't wait either – for the next time at the track.
But it would be a big step, a new beginning. Was he really
ready to take it on? Then he remembered watching Tanni
on the TV and his enthusiasm returned. He decided to go
to the library and see if he could find anything on
Disability Sports, the Paralympics and the National Games
for the Disabled.

The library was about a mile away. This time he
needed to go on his own, to gain some independence, but
he felt nervous as he set off. He took his mobile phone in
case he got stuck. Fortunately, he met with only one
problem when he reached a kerb with no slope, but a
young man came to his rescue and helped him across
the road.

After Jack had struggled through the heavy doors of the
library, he anxiously approached the help desk. Would
they ignore him, or treat him like an imbecile? But he need
not have worried. The librarian was great. To Jack's relief,

she treated him like a normal human being and discussed with him what he might find on the shelves. Together, they searched on her computer and found two books. But it was then that the difficulty arose.

'I'm sorry,' said the librarian. 'The sports section's upstairs.'

'I'd forgotten that,' said Jack. 'I've borrowed sports books before, but I don't think I even noticed that I had to go upstairs to find them.'

'There's no lift, I'm afraid,' said the librarian. 'It's not possible in this old building. Now, if we could have a new library in the town...'

It was a nuisance. He would have liked to browse. There might be other books he could borrow. The librarian fetched the books and Jack set off home. He was feeling tired. He saw a bus pull into the bus stop. That bus would be passing his house in a few minutes, but there was no way he could climb on board. He would never be able to lift himself and his wheelchair up those big steps.

He had to pass the Hobby Shop on the way, so he decided to pop in and buy a new brush for his models. He was pleased to see that Mr Brown had installed a ramp at the door.

'I've brought everything downstairs as I promised,' he said.

'Thanks,' said Jack and he bought some new enamel paints as well as the paint brush.

Then as he trundled along the High Street, he saw an old mate from the football club about 20 metres ahead. He was coming straight towards him. Jack was about to wave and say hello, but the boy dashed across the road and pretended he hadn't seen him. Jack felt as if he had been smacked in the eye.

Why?

He was still fuming when he met up with Kemal's mum.

'Oh, he's not worth worrying about,' said Mrs Unel. 'Perhaps you should feel sorry for him.'

'Me? Feel sorry for him?'

'Well,' said Mrs Unel. 'He's the one who can't face up to you. He's the one with the problem.'

Put like that, Jack supposed he could see what she meant.

'You'll come in for a cuppa,' she said.

Jack smiled. 'OK,' he said. Mrs Unel had always been friendly like that. The trouble was, if you went for a cuppa, you ended up eating a plate of cakes and loads of fruit. She wouldn't take no for an answer.

But when they arrived and made their way to the rear of the greengrocer's shop, they stopped and looked at each other. They had both forgotten that the Unel flat was upstairs above the shop.

'Oh, dear,' said Mrs Unel when they arrived at the bottom of the stairs. 'I'm sorry, Jack. I—'

'Is that you, Mum?' Jack heard Kemal's voice from above.

'Yes, and Jack's with me.'

Kemal leapt downstairs three at a time. Mrs Unel turned to Jack. 'You can't get up there, can you? I'll bring you a cup down here.'

'I'll come up,' said Jack.

He wheeled to the bottom of the stairs, stood up, swivelled himself round and sat on the third step up. He was thankful for the strength in his arms as he pulled himself up step by step until he had reached the top. Later, several kilos heavier, after Mrs Unel's generous hospitality, he reached the bottom and hurried home, carrying a bag of fruit.

It was early evening when Mr Wallis and Jack entered the sports club. It was the one he had been to from the hospital, but it was different this time. There were plenty of athletes there. Some were in wheelchairs like him, but there were people with other disabilities as well. Jack looked all around. Part of him felt pleased to know he wasn't the only one with a disability, but couldn't help wishing he didn't have to be there. If only he could be...

'Hi, Jack.' A man came and shook his hand. 'I'm Terry. I've been talking to Sarah. She says your friend Eliot is coming to join us, too.'

'Soon,' said Jack, feeling his doubts slowly fading away. 'I want to train hard for racing big time.'

'That's what I like to hear,' said Terry. 'I'll be coaching you and I'll expect nothing but 100 per cent commitment.'

'Fine,' said Jack.

The training was harder even than Sarah's regime and Jack went home exhausted after each session. But he knew it was doing him good. Although he still missed football, he found he could think about it more easily without getting upset.

Gradually, Jack was getting used to his new life. Every day, he had to go through his basic routines of emptying his bowel and bladder regularly and searching the paralysed parts of his body all the time to check for pressure sores. He didn't like any of these things, but he knew he had to do them and reluctantly accepted them as another fact of life. But sometimes, there were other problems to face – travelling, for example.

One Saturday, he desperately wanted to go to London on the train for an away game, but there was a step and an enormous gap to climb into the train. Anyway, he knew that the Underground in London would be impossible. You can't get up an escalator in a wheelchair and the station he needed had no lift. So, no trip to London. It was disappointing.

But there were plenty of positive things he could think of when he was feeling depressed, like going to the sports club and training. He was looking forward to competing with Eliot.

`Out of hospital,` Eliot sent a message. `See you at club.`

`When?`

`Next week.`

Eliot and he were going to get on fine. He wondered if Eliot would ever be as close a buddy as Daz and Kemal. He was so glad those two hadn't forgotten him, after all. They were always round at his house listening to music or playing computer games and they were planning their next trip to a home match.

'Have I told you about Eliot?' Jack asked them one evening.

Daz did a fake yawn and fell flat on the bed.

'Only a million times!' said Kemal.

'All right,' laughed Jack. 'For the millionth and one time, he's out of hospital. You'll have to meet him some time.'

'Why not?' said Kemal.

The door opened and Lara breezed in.

'Hi, your sister let me in,' she said as she handed Jack an envelope.

'What's this?'

'It's from Mr Oakley,' said Lara. 'We've been back at school a week now.'

'Misses me, does he?'

'Yeah, I suppose he does.'

Jack thought about that. He supposed he missed Mr Oakley, too.

'You can warn him I'll be back soon,' said Jack. 'But tell him I've got better things to do first.'

'Like what?' asked Lara.

'Like going to Alton Towers,' said Jack. 'Apparently wheelchair users get to jump queues for the best rides. We're going at the weekend.'

Chapter Twelve

It was a long drive to Staffordshire, but Jack was determined he was going to have a perfect day. He settled down next to Craig in the back of the car, wondering how they were going to get on.

But soon Craig began to chatter. He went on and on about his computer and what he planned to do when he left school, then he began on the jokes.

'Hey! What's that copper doing up that tree?'

Jack said nothing. That was an old one!

'He's working for special branch!'

They passed a field of sheep. Jack somehow knew the one about the criminal sheep was next. Craig was beginning to drive him mad. He couldn't get a word in edgeways. It was really weird. Craig had taken over his role.

Let him, he thought. *I don't care.*

But he did care. The trouble was the louder Craig became, the more Jack crept into his shell. By the time they were halfway there, he was feeling he wouldn't be able to stand a whole day with Craig. At last, their dad stopped the car and turned round in his seat.

'For goodness sake, Craig!' he said. 'You'll drive us all bananas!'

Jack grinned at his dad, but Craig shut up like a clam and remained silent, in a sulk for the rest of the journey. When they arrived at the amusement park, Jack watched Craig out of the corner of his eye. It was amazing how his kid brother had grown up in the last few months. He was taller, but he had also become much more confident.

The rides were fantastic. And it was a bonus not having to queue for hours for each one, but they didn't speak to each other. Jack presumed Craig was still smarting from their dad's outburst, but he couldn't think of anything to say to break the deadlock. At last, it was Craig who spoke first. They were hurrying to the next ride when he suddenly stopped and stood right in front of the wheelchair.

'Queue-jumping's fine,' he said. 'Thank goodness there's one decent thing happening round here.'

'What do you mean?' Jack demanded, jamming his hands on the wheels to avoid running his brother down.

Craig shifted uncomfortably from one foot to the other. 'Well,' he said, avoiding looking at Jack. 'It's been bad.'

'Don't I know it?' said Jack.

'Yeah, for you,' said Craig. 'We all know it's been terrible for you, but—'

'But what?'

'You haven't thought about what it's like for us, have you?'

'I ... well, Emma did say something...'

Crowds of people surged past them, but Craig didn't seem to notice.

'It's been Jack this and Jack that,' he said. 'And oh no, we can't come and see the work you've done on your computer. We've got to go and see Jack. You'll be OK to get your own meals for the next five months, won't you? We've just got to turn the house upside down, if that's all right by you.'

Jack swallowed the lump in his throat. He should have realised, especially after what Emma had said. Craig had been through a difficult time, too.

'I'm sorry,' he said. 'Only I didn't intend to throw everyone into this. I've been so devastated by what happened to me, I just haven't thought about the rest of you. It must have been hell for everyone.'

Craig's eyes were full of tears as he looked down at Jack.

'I shouldn't have said all that,' he said.

'Yes, you should,' said Jack. 'How will I know if you don't say?'

'I feel better though, now it's out in the open.'

'Come on, we're missing our next ride.'

By the end of the day, Jack felt he was beginning to get to know his brother, and it felt good.

From then on, Jack was so busy, he hardly noticed the days flashing by. The next time he went to the athletics club, Eliot was there. After fitness training they wheeled down to the track with three other boys.

'OK,' said Terry. 'Let's see what you're made of.'

They sped round one lap of the track. Jack came in third. He was gasping for breath and he could hear the blood pounding through his head. He was disgusted with himself.

'I thought I was fit,' he wheezed. 'I'll win next time!'

Eliot had come in last.

'Not if I can help it!' he panted.

'We'll work on your racing technique,' Terry said. 'You're a determined young man, Jack Wallis. You'll get there in the end, I can see.'

It was time to return to school. Jack had mixed feelings about it. He was dying to see everyone and he needed something to occupy him. He was getting bored at home. But he was terrified. How would they all react to him? How would he fit in? The necessary changes to the school had been completed. A visit had been arranged.

One morning, Jack wheeled himself nervously into the school entrance hall. The place seemed dead. Everyone was in lessons. Good. It gave him a few minutes to prepare himself, to get used to being here again. Then suddenly, a bell rang. Jack almost leapt out of his wheelchair. His heart pounded in his chest. He had barely had time to recover when crowds poured into the entrance hall. It was break.

He was surrounded by strangers. It seemed that the entire school knew all about his fall and his injuries. He was patted on the shoulders, kissed by loads of girls and his hand ached for being shaken so many times. He felt totally confused. His brain went into panic mode. He wanted to back out, disappear, get right away. He recognised nobody. Where were his friends?

Then, one by one, familiar faces appeared. Daz pushed through the crowds, then Lara and Kemal.

'Jack's back!' he heard whispered around him.

Suddenly, he felt like a film star. He smiled. They want me back, he thought. It isn't going to be so bad.

After break, his form was due in the gym.

'Why don't you come with us?' said Kemal. 'Old Oakley will be pleased to see you. Anyway, it's basketball.'

Basketball! Jack didn't need a second invitation.

'OK,' he said. 'I'll come.'

He was pleased to find that ramps had been placed at the side of each set of steps and at all the entrances so he had no trouble making his way to the gym.

'Oh no! Not Jack Wallis!' said Mr Oakley, shaking his hand warmly. 'Don't say you're back with us already?'

'Next week,' said Jack, 'I'll be here pestering you again.'

The basketball game began. Jack sat on the sidelines and watched, but suddenly the ball flew high towards him. He stretched up and snatched it out of the air, set his wheelchair in motion and zigzagged across the gym, bouncing the ball in front of him until he was under the basket.

The ball shot through the basket. It felt great. The buzz was still there.

'I might have known you'd cause a stir the moment you turned up!' laughed Mr Oakley.

Jack grinned up at his teacher. He enjoyed basketball, but his ambition was on the athletics track now.

It was only a few weeks later that Jack sat in lane in his new sports wheelchair, his eyes focussed on the way ahead. He and Eliot had been training hard several times a week, pumping weights, building up their muscles. Terry had been a great help showing them the best way to work on the wheels of the chair and they had raced against each other many times. So far, Jack had always reached the line first, but Eliot was getting stronger all the time. It was different when they raced other people. Jack hadn't managed to win a race yet. But he loved the competition. He was always desperate to win.

Now they were about to start their first big race. Eliot was on the lane inside him, but all eight lanes were being used. That meant seven to beat!

As Jack had rolled down the ramp onto the track a few minutes earlier, he had glanced up at the stand, encouraged by the fact that he knew his parents were there with Daz, Kemal and Lara and several other friends from school. He had imagined he could hear Lara shouting, but there was so much noise he couldn't be sure.

The crowd was suddenly silent. The starter was in position, raising his pistol. Jack bent forward, his hands gripping the wheel, ready for the first spurt of energy that was needed to propel the chair along the track.

'On your marks...'

Bang!

Jack felt the surge of adrenalin rushing through his body as he began to race. He was already up on the boy outside him, but he was aware of Eliot close behind. He could hear his heavy breathing as they shot round the first bend. Soon they were halfway round. He was well up with the rest. Could he pull it off – in his first real race?

He was panting hard. His muscles ached now as his chest heaved. Every metre was more difficult. They rounded the second bend into the home straight. The winning tape was ahead, but Jack was tiring. He just had to keep going.

'Come on, Jack!' Lara and Brook screamed from the stand.

'Come on, Jack!' he echoed in his brain. 'You can do it!'

There were two athletes ahead of him, but Jack could see that one of them was fading and he passed him with ease. Now there was one more to beat. The tape was close now. Could he do it?

Jack shot past the winning post just behind the leader. He sat hunched in his chair, gasping for breath, but feeling great. Second wasn't what he had aimed at, but there would be a next time. He would train even harder and win.

And one day, Olympic Champion? Why not?

If you enjoyed reading *You Can Do It!*, look out for the next title in the *Go For It!* series: *No Way!* by Sue Vyner.

● ● ● ● ● ● ● ● ● ● ● ● ● ● ● ● ●

She had really been looking forward to seeing this film. But as soon as it started, Mum and *him* got closer. Leaning against each other.

Jessie began to drink her coke making a loud sucking noise through the straw.

That did the trick. Mum leaned away from Steve and towards her, then frowned disapprovingly. Like when Jessie was little. Making Jessie make all the more noise. Like she was little. When Mum frowned at her again, it made her giggle nervously.

Mum definitely wasn't amused. A kid a few seats away was, though. She giggled too, then did the same thing with her drink.

Mum leaned over Jessie. 'You're showing yourself up,' she whispered.

She was showing herself up? When Mum had been sitting there nearly on his knee! That made Jessie really mad. Well. If Mum thought she was showing herself up, she may as well live up to it. She flicked some popcorn over the heads of the row in front.

A kid looked round and flicked some back.

'Stop it,' Mum hissed. 'Stop it, Jessie.'

Steve got hold of Mum's hand and squeezed it as if to say take no notice of her.

Jessie longed to tell him to get off her mum.

By now she'd lost the gist of the film. And it felt like she had the devil in her. She slid down the seat, folded her arms, and put her feet up on the seat in front of her. Like she'd seen others do.

Mum leaned over and pushed them down.

Jessie thought she saw a glint in Steve's eye. Was he going to do a *dad* on her at last? Then Mum would see him for what he was? She put her feet up again.

A man turned round. 'Put your feet down!' he demanded in the middle of a dramatic moment in the film.

A woman along the row shushed.

People were turning round. Looking.

Jessie wished she could sink down into the seat and disappear. She wanted to curl up and die. She hated being the centre of attention.

The film was ruined. And all because of *him*.